BEYOND THE SUNRISE

'It's just a little further,' said Jody over her shoulder.

'But what if there are snakes?' Brittany whimpered.

Philip reached out and took her hand. 'No snakes are going to get you,' he said reassuringly.

Brittany blushed. Then she gave a wobbly smile, and fell silent. Jody decided that Philip was a very useful influence on Brittany's theatrical nerves.

Shiv came to an abrupt stop at the end of the path. 'There,' he said, pointing.

The boat was still bobbing gently in the water channel in front of them.

Philip whistled. 'That's some machine,' he said admiringly. 'But what on earth is it doing here?'

'That's what we want to know,' Jody agreed, frowning.

Dolphin Diaries™

BEYOND THE SUNRISE
Lucy Daniels

Hodder
Children's
Books

a division of Hodder Headline Limited

Special thanks to Lucy Courtenay

Thanks also to the Whale and Dolphin Conservation Society for reviewing the information contained in this book

1

May 26 – dawn – Dolphin Dreamer, Sundarbans Delta,
Bangladesh
The sun has only just risen, and the whole river is
beginning to change colour. It was grey about five
minutes ago, and now it's orange and red and pink –
all the colours of the dawn sky. It's an incredible,
beautiful sight.

All the fishermen have been working for nearly an
hour already. Can you believe it? They are as quiet as
anything. I don't think the fish really know that they
are there. The otters don't make any noise either. Yes,
trained otters! I couldn't believe my eyes either! I feel

like the fishermen, Shiv and I are the only people alive. It's magical.

Jody McGrath closed her diary, and stood up. The deck of *Dolphin Dreamer* was cool and slightly damp under her feet as she walked across it as quietly as she could. The river lapped gently at the sides of the boat, and at the roots of the great mangrove trees, gnarled and twisted at the water's edge in the dawn light.

Ten-year-old Shivam Kaushik looked round from his position by *Dolphin Dreamer*'s railings as Jody approached. He had suggested this early-morning adventure yesterday at dinner. He and Jody had slipped out before sunrise to watch the fishermen at work. The deck of *Dolphin Dreamer* gave them a fine view of the action.

'Have I missed much, Shiv?' Jody whispered.

Shiv smiled at her, his white teeth gleaming in the light of the rising sun. 'Not much,' he said. 'Except Jafar's otter just swallowed one of his biggest fish. He wasn't very happy!'

Jody grinned back. The otters weren't supposed to eat the fish. They wore special collars to stop them swallowing anything too big. Jafar's otter must have lost his collar. Jody knew that she should sympathize with the fishermen, because losing fish meant losing money. But she couldn't help feeling glad that the hard-working otter had sneaked a reward for all his work.

They watched the otters as they slid off the brightly-coloured fishermen's houseboats and into the smooth water of the river with hardly a splash. The sleek silver fish grouped together nervously just below the surface of the water – sensing the presence of hunters. The otters then chased the fish straight into the waiting nets. It was a wonderful sight.

The fishermen were shouting, hauling their catches out of the water. They pulled them in, hand over hand, until the full nets of gleaming, wriggling silver and black hit the decks of their long, low, brightly-painted boats. The catch was good that morning, Jody could tell.

The Sundarbans Delta was a maze of mangrove swamps and rivers in the Bay of Bengal. Part of the Sundarbans lay in India, and the rest in Bangladesh. Hundreds of small rivers cut through the mangroves and down to the sea, most of them stemming from

India's sacred river, the Ganges. It was a strange, watery world, and a UNESCO world heritage site. And most importantly, it was home to a couple of rather unusual species of dolphin, though Jody hadn't seen any yet.

Jody's parents, Craig and Gina McGrath, were marine biologists. They and the rest of their team had arrived in the Sundarbans two days ago, aboard their boat *Dolphin Dreamer*. They were all staying with Shiv's parents, Ravi and Sunnu Kaushik, at the Sukhi Rest House, a smartly thatched hut with a wide wooden veranda which stood a little way back from the river's edge, just behind where *Dolphin Dreamer* was moored.

Dolphin Dreamer had been sailing around the world for almost a year now, researching dolphins in their natural habitats. Jody knew how lucky she was to have been allowed on this trip. She felt like she had increased her knowledge of dolphins a thousand times over since leaving her home in Florida the previous June. She hadn't thought it was possible to love dolphins more than she already did, but the sight of a dolphin, even after nearly a year of seeing them in different places around the world, always made her heart jump with joy.

Jody had made friends with Shiv, the Kaushiks' eldest son, almost as soon as they had arrived at the Sukhi Rest House. Although Shiv was two years younger than Jody, his English was good, thanks to a regular stream of English-speaking visitors, scientists and researchers who stayed at his parents' rest house. He loved to talk to Jody about the wildlife of the Delta, and he was so knowledgeable about the animals in the Sundarbans that Jody was learning something new from him every minute. He, in turn, enjoyed practising his English with Jody, and was keen to learn about the places she had visited and the dolphins she had seen.

Jody glanced at the net on the nearest fishing boat, and frowned. 'Shiv, these nets don't hurt the dolphins, do they?' she asked anxiously.

Jody knew that one of the greatest dangers to dolphins often lay with the kind of nets fishermen used. If the mesh was the wrong size, the dolphins would get caught, and wouldn't be able to escape. Because they needed to breathe above water, they could sometimes even drown as the nets trapped them below the surface.

'The nets are safe,' Shiv assured Jody. 'And the fishermen would never hurt the dolphins. They believe that dolphins are sacred.'

Jody was intrigued. 'You mean, they worship them?'

'Not exactly,' said Shiv. 'But there are stories, you know? Fishermen love stories. I have grown up hearing stories of dolphins.'

'What kind of stories?' asked Jody.

'I have heard of a river with a white dolphin in India,' said Shiv. 'The villagers say that the dolphin is really a young girl. She was in love with a young fisherman, but one day he drowned far out at sea. The girl cried so much that the river rose around her, and she became a dolphin. Perhaps she sees her fisherman now, down at the bottom of the sea.'

'That's sad,' said Jody after a moment. She pictured the lonely white dolphin in the river.

'We have happy stories too,' Shiv added. 'South of here, I have heard that dolphins help fishermen to catch the fish, like otters!' He pointed at the otters, which were standing on the decks of the fishing boats, watching their owners sort the catch and waiting for their reward.

'Or sheepdogs,' said Jody.

Shiv nodded. 'I have heard of this,' he said. 'The dogs chase the sheep, yes?'

'They don't chase them!' Jody laughed. 'At least, they aren't supposed to. They herd them.'

'I have never seen a sheep,' said Shiv. 'I have seen pictures, though. They must be very hot in their wool coats.'

'They often live in pretty cold countries,' Jody pointed out. 'They need their coats for the winter.'

Shiv smiled and shrugged. For all his local knowledge, he knew very little about life outside the Delta. He had spent his whole life in the Sundarbans, and all the information he had about other places in the world came from the few books his parents had in the house and the visitors he had spoken to. Jody knew that he found it difficult to understand the idea of really cold weather. In the Sundarbans, the mangrove swamps kept the air moist, and temperatures never fell below freezing. Most of the year the Delta air was heavy, hot and humid. Today was no exception.

'Maybe one day the dolphins in this river will help the Sundarbans fishermen,' said Shiv hopefully.

'I have never seen it, but if it happens in the south, it can happen here, I am sure of it. Today the catch was good, but I have seen days where the fishermen catch very little.'

'Do you have white dolphins here in the Sundarbans?' Jody asked.

'I have never seen a white one,' said Shiv. 'We have Ganges river dolphins, which are grey. Also Irrawaddy dolphins.'

Irrawaddy dolphins! These were the dolphins Jody was hoping to see. Her parents had told her all about them – they were famous for keeping a low profile. She had seen a few pictures of Irrawaddies, and she thought that they looked adorable. Their heads were blunt and rounded, without beaks, which made them look both friendly and faintly comical.

'Have you ever seen an Irrawaddy dolphin?' Jody asked eagerly.

Shiv nodded. 'Of course,' he said with a laugh. 'But not many. Ganges dolphins and Irrawaddies are very rare.'

A sudden worrying thought struck Jody. 'Shiv,' she said. 'We're only staying for ten days, and we've already been here for two of those. Do you think we'll see an Irrawaddy?'

'Maybe,' said Shiv. 'You just have to look very hard. They don't often jump out of the river, so they are not so easy to see.'

Jody remembered reading about the Irrawaddy habit of keeping below the river surface. Irrawaddies were totally unlike bottlenose dolphins, which happily leaped above the water for the world to see. She resolved to keep a very sharp eye on the river, just in case she caught one gliding past. 'They must come up to breathe,' she said hopefully. 'Maybe we'll see one breathing.'

'It's possible,' Shiv agreed. 'But they like to be somewhere quiet and safe when they come up for air. You should be prepared not to see one, maybe. Then you won't be disappointed.'

Jody frowned. The Irrawaddy sounded even more of a challenge than some of the other notoriously shy dolphins she had managed to see over the past year. The Indo-Pacific humpback dolphin didn't show itself very often, although she had managed to make friends with one in Australia. And the river botos of South America had been very secretive as well. She knew that seeing a shy dolphin had a special thrill of its own, but she wished that it was a little easier. They had been lucky so far, but maybe the Irrawaddy would be the first dolphin to stay out of sight?

'It may not be so bad,' said Shiv, relenting at the sight of Jody's thoughtful face. 'The Irrawaddy is curious, like other dolphins. Sometimes they put their heads above the water, like this.' He bobbed his head up to imitate a dolphin rising to the surface of a river to take a look around.

Jody laughed. 'Like a seal!' she said.

'A seal?' said Shivam. 'What is a seal?'

Jody explained. It was amazing to think that Shivam had never seen a seal, or even a picture of a seal. It struck her again just how lucky she was to be on this trip, travelling around the world and experiencing so much.

They both turned round when they heard footsteps behind them.

'You two are up early,' yawned Harry Pierce, coming up the cabin steps to join Jody and Shiv on the deck.

Harry was the captain of *Dolphin Dreamer*, and

had decided to sleep aboard the ship while they were in the Sundarbans. When the McGraths had tried to persuade him to join them at the Sukhi Rest House, he had explained that he didn't sleep very well on dry land. He missed the rocking motion of the boat. Harry's daughter, Brittany, who was also on the trip, had no such problems. She had been the first off the *Dolphin Dreamer* when they had docked, and she had bagged the best bed in the rest house. Unlike Jody, she wasn't a big fan of life at sea.

'Was it a good catch?' Harry asked, shading his eyes and looking out at the fishing boats.

'It seemed pretty good,' Jody began.

Suddenly, the calm waters at the side of the boat began to boil as something below the surface thrashed a huge tail. A flock of brightly-coloured birds rose from the mangrove trees in alarm, flapping their wings in a riot of colour and noise.

'What's happening?' Jody asked in surprise.

The water calmed down again. Minutes later, it foamed around the base of the fishing boats, and turned a murky brown. The fishermen yelled and ducked inside the cabins on the boats.

11

'Look!' Shiv suddenly shouted, pointing into the water.

Jody stared in horror as a long, dark body rose out of the river, opening a pair of huge jaws. A crocodile!

A crocodile causes chaos . . .

2

May 26 – midday – upstairs in the Sukhi Rest House
I've never seen such a huge crocodile as the one we
saw this morning. It made the alligators back home in
Florida look like toys! It must have been as long as one
of the houseboats moored along the edge of the river. It
gave us such a shock. It managed to catch one of the
nets, which was still trailing in the water. We watched
as it dragged the net, with all its fish, back into the
river. The fisherman didn't stand a chance of pulling
the net back on board. If he'd tried, the croc would have
pulled him overboard as well.

Shiv says the net belonged to Jafar – the same

fisherman whose otter ate the biggest fish. All in all, poor old Jafar had a pretty bad day's fishing.

Jody looked up from her diary with a yawn. Her bed was very comfortable – she'd almost fallen asleep halfway through her description of the morning she had shared with Shiv and the fishermen. But she had been determined to finish her entry before lunch.

The diary had been her father's idea. He had kept a diary when he was a boy, and had even won a competition with his writing. When they had left Florida the previous June, he had suggested to Jody that she might like to keep a special diary of all the places they visited.

A year later and the notebook was a bit dirtier round the edges, but it was steadily filling up. Jody loved taking a little time every day to think about the things she had seen and write them down. Her diary had become like a friend, someone she could chat to and confide in. She knew that when they returned to Florida, it would be a fantastic reminder of the trip.

She put the diary down on the wooden bedside

table and stood up, breathing in the rich smell of the warm, wooden walls around her. She was sharing the room with Brittany. There was a fine-meshed mosquito net in the window, which faced away from the river, and two more nets draped around the beds. Brightly-patterned curtains and a rag rug on the floor finished the picture, along with a wonderful, mysterious view of the dark and tangled Sundarbans forest out of the window. It made quite a change from the wide, blue, sea view from Jody's cabin aboard *Dolphin Dreamer*.

As she slipped on her shoes, Jody thought about the unlucky fisherman they'd seen that morning. Back home, losing a fishing net was no big deal. You just had to go to the nearest store and buy a new one. But here, it was very different. The fishermen made their own nets, which could take several days. Several days making a net meant several days without catching any fish. And no fish meant no money. Jody hoped that the fisherman didn't have a big family to feed.

From what Jody had seen, the Sundarbans people had a hard life. Most of them earned their living as fishermen, catching fish and shellfish. Others worked as woodcutters, or honey collectors. Tourism was limited, the climate was wet and unpredictable, and the area was full of wild and dangerous animals. But somehow, the people were both cheerful and welcoming.

Jody made her way downstairs, to join the rest of the family. The spiced smell of cooking rice reminded her that breakfast had been a long time ago.

Shiv greeted her with a broad smile. 'Jafar has found his net,' he announced as Jody came into the room. 'It arrived on the bank, floating very near Jafar's boat. Chalaka didn't like the taste, I think!'

'Good!' said Jody with relief. Then she frowned. 'Chalaka?' she said curiously. 'Is that the name of the crocodile?'

'Chalaka means "clever" in Hindi,' said Shiv's father. He was a slim, short man with dark wings of hair which fell neatly either side of a parting. In his arms, he was holding the sleeping form of three-year-old Ambika, the Kaushiks' youngest daughter. 'That crocodile is very clever, so Chalaka is her name. The fishermen know her well. But I think she knows *them* even better!'

'Come and eat.' Shiv's mother, Sunnu, beckoned Jody to the table, where the rest of her family, plus Brittany, were sitting.

'About time!' said Jimmy with relief. 'I'm starving!'

Jimmy was one of Jody's brothers, and was permanently hungry.

'Me too,' said Sean, Jimmy's twin. '*Starving*.'

With their red hair and fair freckled skin, the two eight-year-old boys looked very like their father, whereas Jody took after her darker-skinned Italian mother, Gina.

'Sorry everyone,' Jody said, sitting down next to her mother. 'I was writing about the crocodile Shiv and I saw this morning. You should have been there!'

'I couldn't get out of bed this morning,' said Gina McGrath apologetically. 'It must be our bed, Sunnu. It's the most comfortable thing I've slept in since we left Florida!'

Sunnu smiled at the compliment, and placed a dish of rice on the table. Jimmy immediately reached for it, but Jody's dad was too quick for him.

'Oh no, you don't,' he said swiftly, batting away

his son's greedy fingers. 'You can wait your turn, like everyone else.'

'Please, help yourself!' Sunnu laughed. She was a short, plump woman with slanting, almond-shaped eyes and a long, shining plait down her back. 'It's good to see hungry boys.'

'I'm glad I didn't see a crocodile,' said Brittany Pierce with a shiver, reaching for the pile of warm, fragrant chapatis that had been placed in the middle of the table. 'I would have screamed.'

'You always scream,' said Jimmy, and pulled a face at her. 'Even at the titchiest creepy-crawly.'

Sean sniggered.

'Ha, ha,' Brittany said sarcastically, flipping her wavy fair hair back over her shoulders. 'You are so not funny, Jimmy.'

Brittany had joined *Dolphin Dreamer* at the last minute back in June, when her mother had unexpectedly gone to Europe on holiday. Harry Pierce hadn't planned on having his daughter along on the trip, but there had been no alternative. She had been a difficult member of the team from that first day, when she had made it very clear that she didn't want to be there. Even though she had changed a lot in the last year, she was still very easy to tease.

Jody looked round. 'Where are the others?' she asked.

'Let's see,' said Gina, counting on her fingers. 'Harry's on the boat, as you know. Cam's with him.'

Cameron Tucker was *Dolphin Dreamer*'s first mate, and Harry's right-hand man.

'Mei Lin was invited to lunch by one of the fishing families today,' Gina continued.

'I hope she gets a few recipes while she's there,' Craig joked, reaching for the rice and piling it high on his plate. 'With any luck we'll get a few local dishes on the next leg of our trip.'

Mei Lin Zhong was *Dolphin Dreamer*'s cook, though she had been an engineering student back in China.

'I have no idea where Maddie is,' Gina admitted. 'Maybe preparing your next algebra lesson.' She winked at Jody and her brothers.

Jody, Sean and Jimmy all groaned. They loved Maddie, their fun young tutor, but algebra was algebra, whether you were in Florida or Bangladesh.

'And . . .' Gina paused and frowned. 'Oh, who have I forgotten?'

'Dr Taylor,' said Jimmy and Sean in unison.

'As if you could forget Dr Taylor,' sighed Brittany.

'Did somebody call?' A pink, balding head appeared around the door. Dr Jefferson Taylor peered in from the veranda, blinking in the dim light. He was the representative of *Dolphin Dreamer*'s sponsor, PetroCo, and had been with the expedition from the beginning. 'I'm just rather caught up here with what I believe is a grey-headed fish eagle.' He waved a pair of binoculars to emphasize his point. 'Just as well we found these,' he said. 'Though I must say, finding them in my laundry basket was a little unexpected. How they got there, I'll never know.' He looked outside again. 'Most rare, the grey-headed fish eagle,' he muttered with satisfaction, before vanishing from sight.

Jimmy and Sean burst out laughing. Jody couldn't help grinning either. The Kaushiks' younger son, Ajay, had confessed to hiding Dr Taylor's binoculars that morning. He had been sent up to his room over an hour ago, to think about his crime. At seven years old, he was as naughty as the twins, and the three boys were already firm friends.

A moment later Dr Taylor reappeared. 'I'm so sorry,' he said. 'I quite forgot to ask. Was I called in for a reason?'

Gina smiled at him. 'Not to worry, Dr Taylor. Lunch is here, when you feel like it.'

'Most kind,' nodded Dr Taylor. 'One does work up quite an appetite when bird-watching. Just one moment . . .'

And as if he was being pulled by an invisible string, Dr Taylor disappeared outside again.

Lunch was almost over when an unexpected visitor arrived at the door.

'Harry!' said Gina. 'I didn't think we were ever going to get you ashore! Would you like some lunch?'

Harry pulled a face, and scratched absently at his beard. 'I'm not hungry, thanks, Gina.'

Jody saw that the captain was looking worried.

Craig noticed as well. 'What's up, Harry?' he asked. 'Is there a problem?'

'The *Dolphin Dreamer*'s engine has been leaking

oil all morning,' Harry replied. 'I think we've got a problem with the carburetor.'

'Oh dear, can it be fixed?' asked Gina, concern in her voice.

The captain shook his head. 'I don't think so this time. The carburetor is pretty much worn out after that long trek from Australia. Cam took a look and he agrees. We're going to have to replace it before we leave, or we could find ourselves stranded in the middle of the Indian Ocean.'

'Don't we keep spare parts aboard?' asked Craig.

Harry nodded. 'Of course. But unfortunately, we need more than just spare parts. I'm going to need to find a boatyard pretty fast, or we'll end up staying here longer than we planned. If we're still here when the monsoon season starts, well . . .'

He didn't need to finish his sentence. Monsoon weather, with its lashing rain and howling winds, was notoriously bad in this part of the world. Jody knew how important it was that they left the Sundarbans before the monsoon, or they could well be stranded in Bangladesh for several months. It was vital that they kept to their schedule, or they could miss seeing certain species of dolphin altogether.

There was a brief, worried silence.

'Is there a boatyard near here, Ravi?' said Craig at last, turning to their host. 'I mean a big boatyard, one that's equipped to fix major problems like this?'

'Not right here,' said Ravi. 'But you have seen the Sundarbans. Boats are a way of life to us. We depend on them for everything. So yes, we have some good boatyards.' He thought for a moment. 'I would suggest Mongla, perhaps. It is a three-hour journey up the Pusur river. Can your boat make a trip like that?'

Harry looked relieved. 'I'm sure we have several more hours of use left in the carburetor, if we don't push the engine too fast. I think we should head to Mongla in the morning.'

'I will telephone ahead now, to make sure that the yard knows you are coming,' said Sunnu. 'Khaled is the owner, we know him. I am sure that he will be able to do the work for you.'

'Thank you so much,' said Gina with relief. 'We really can't stay here into the monsoon season. Much as we'd love to stay in the Sundarbans for a few more months, Sunnu, we . . .'

Sunnu waved her hand. 'I know. The world is a

big place, and you must travel when you can. We would like to have you for longer as well, but monsoon is a bad time. I think you won't like the Sundarbans as much then as perhaps you do now!'

'Maybe you will see your Irrawaddy dolphin tomorrow,' said Shiv, as he guided his small wooden dinghy away from the Sukhi mooring that afternoon. 'The Pusur is a great river, and many animals live in it. Three hours to Mongla and three hours back is plenty of time for you to look.'

'I hope so,' Jody said fervently. She looked at the swirling brown river which flowed around them. 'I might even see an Irrawaddy now!'

'And if you don't see an Irrawaddy, I promise you will see plenty of other exciting things instead,' said Shiv confidently.

He steered the boat into calmer water. He was taking Jody out to explore the mangrove forest. He had offered to take Brittany as well, but she'd taken one look at his small, battered dinghy and refused to set foot in it. So once again, he and Jody were on their own.

Because the forest was made up of many hundreds

of small islands, the only way to travel was by boat. Jody loved the idea of sailing through a forest. It reminded her of the Orinoco river delta in South America, where the boto dolphins had sometimes swum among the tree branches when the river level was high enough.

Jody looked around her at Shiv's boat. It was a little shabby, but it was also watertight, and surprisingly comfortable. 'Does your dinghy have a name, Shiv?' she asked.

Shiv looked pleased at the question. 'She is called *Big Ben*,' he said proudly. 'I have always wanted to see London, and so I have a piece of London here at home with me.'

'It's a good name,' Jody smiled. 'And London's a pretty good place, I hear. I'd love to go there some day too.'

They started talking about the places Jody had visited. Soon, they were so caught up in their conversation that Jody forgot to watch out for dolphins.

Suddenly, halfway through a conversation about the pilot whales in the Canary Islands, Shiv touched Jody's sleeve.

'Look,' he said. 'Fishing cat.'

A large wildcat with spotted, olive-grey fur was crouched on the shore, watching them. Jody stared back with awe. The fishing cat's wild amber eyes glowed at them for a moment before it turned its attention to the river. Suddenly, it flashed a paw into the water, and hooked a large, wriggling eel out with a powerful claw. With one final suspicious glance over its shoulder at Jody and Shiv, the cat slipped into the forest to enjoy its feast.

Fishing cat

They saw plenty of other exciting things that afternoon, as Shiv had promised. Screeching monkeys swung over their heads through the narrower river channels, and long-legged river waders picked their way delicately along the muddy river shore. They even saw a sleeping python hanging among the branches of a tree. There didn't seem to be any crocodiles in this part of the river, Jody was thankful to see.

Suddenly, a rounded grey shape rose briefly out of the water, just ahead of the dinghy. It vanished again a second later.

'Shiv, I think that was a dolphin!' Jody breathed, pointing. 'Follow it, quick!'

The dolphin breached again, very briefly. It was breaking the surface of the water for only a moment. Jody narrowed her eyes, trying to pick out a distinctive head shape. Was it an Irrawaddy?

They followed the dolphin's wake towards a small, mossy-looking island. It darted suddenly into one of a tangle of water channels, and Jody lost sight of it.

'It's OK,' said Shiv, guiding the dinghy down the channel. 'I think if we land, we will be able to follow it on foot.'

They bumped gently ashore, beside a clump of tall, dark green bamboo, which rose up as straight and high as a building. Shiv lashed the dinghy to the gnarled stump of a mangrove tree, and hopped ashore. Then he held a finger to his lips, and beckoned Jody to cross the island with him, towards a water channel on the opposite side.

'Hey!' an angry voice shouted. 'What are you doing? You should not be here. You must leave!'

A very tall, dark-skinned man was standing there, glaring furiously at Jody. Jody nearly leapt out of her skin at the sound of his voice.

The man took a step towards her. 'Go away!' he said again, flapping his hands. 'You are trespassing. Go away!'

Shiv stepped forward and asked the man a question in Hindi. The man replied in a furious burst of language, waving his hands and shouting. He was clearly very upset.

'Shiv, I think we should go,' said Jody in a low voice, backing towards the dinghy.

Shiv turned to her. 'This is not right,' he said. 'He does not own this land. He cannot tell us to leave.'

28

The man was still shouting. He took a threatening step towards them.

Jody pulled at Shiv's arm. 'Come on, Shiv,' she said. 'We can come back another day.'

The man swung back to her. 'No,' he said clearly. 'No other day. You must leave, and not come back.'

He obviously wasn't going to change his mind. Jody pulled Shiv back to the dinghy, and they cast off. The tall man stood on the shore of the island, and watched them leave.

'Don't think you can sneak back!' he shouted across the water. 'I will speak to your parents, Shivam Kaushik. I want a promise that you will never trespass on my land again!'

3

Jody and Shiv found their parents sitting on the veranda of the Sukhi Rest House when they got back. Ajay and the boys were playing inside, and little Ambika was sitting at Sunnu's feet, playing with a doll and singing quietly to herself. Brittany was playing cards with Maddie, and Dr Taylor was at the table making careful notes about the birds he had seen that day. Jody suddenly felt very glad to see so many friendly faces.

'Did you have a good trip?' asked Craig, looking up.

'Yes and no,' Jody admitted, sitting beside him.

'We saw a fishing cat, which was fantastic. And we spotted a dolphin, but then we met this horrible man who chased us away.'

'It was Mr Vikram,' Shiv explained to his parents. 'He shouted at us because he said we were trespassing. But we were nowhere near his land.'

'Shiv,' said Sunnu, 'remember. This is Mr Vikram we are talking about. He doesn't follow the same rules as the rest of us.'

'Why not?' Jody wanted to know.

Ravi swung thoughtfully on the veranda seat, which was piled high with creamy cushions. 'Mr Vikram is a neighbour of ours,' he said. 'He is a strange man, but you shouldn't worry about him. He has lived alone since his wife died last year, and he has become very solitary. We have learned just to leave him alone. Perhaps it is wisest for you to do the same.'

Jody thought it sounded very sad. 'Did he love his wife very much?' she asked.

'Yes,' said Sunnu. 'He did.'

A strange noise from the depths of the forest made Jody turn her head. It sounded like a deep, throaty cough.

Ravi and Sunnu immediately stood up, and looked out into the trees. Jody's parents did the same.

'What was that?' Jody asked curiously.

'Tiger,' said Ravi, his eyes searching the forest.

Brittany shrieked and dropped her cards.

'It's OK,' Sunnu reassured her. 'It won't come to the rest house. But it might be better if we went inside anyway.'

Everyone obediently moved into the house.

'This place is so dangerous!' Brittany complained, throwing herself down on one of the sofas in the main living area. 'First crocodiles, and now tigers!'

'Tigers?' Jimmy asked with interest, looking up from his board game with Sean and Ajay. 'Cool!'

'Not very cool if you are facing a hungry one, Jimmy,' said Gina dryly.

'I faced a hungry tiger once,' boasted Ajay.

'Yes – and the door was locked and the window was closed!' Sunnu teased, ruffling her son's hair.

'You may see tigers tomorrow, on the way to Mongla,' said Ravi. 'There are maybe three hundred in the Bangladeshi part of the Sundarbans.'

'And if you don't see the tiger,' Sunnu added, smiling, 'the tiger will most certainly see you. There is a saying in the Sundarbans, "Here the Tiger is always watching you".'

'I don't mind if the tiger is watching,' said Brittany. 'So long as that's all it's doing.'

'And what about dolphins?' Jody asked hopefully.

'I was about to ask the same thing!' laughed Gina. 'We've been here for two days already, and we haven't laid eyes on the purpose of our visit.'

'The *porpoise* of our visit,' Sean quipped, and Jimmy collapsed into giggles.

A tall, fair-haired young man stepped into the room, and looked around. His loose linen clothes were streaked with paint, and he had a splodge of blue on his left cheek. 'New guests, I see?' he said with a smile.

'Philip, at last you are here!' Sunnu exclaimed. 'I wondered if our other guests would ever have the chance to meet you.' She introduced the young man as Philip Warner, a visiting wildlife artist who had been staying with the Kaushiks for the past six months. He'd been up the coast for three days, studying some loggerhead turtles there. He had an engaging manner, and Jody liked him immediately.

So did Brittany, judging from the way she blushed when he shook her hand.

'So, you're all off to Mongla tomorrow, are you?' he enquired, having been filled in on the day's events. 'It's market day, so you should have fun. Sadly I can't join you – I'm heading into the forest to find a tiger.'

'You won't have to go very far,' said Brittany. 'We just heard one outside.' She tried to sound excited by the thought, rather than scared.

Philip's eyes brightened. 'Great,' he said. 'On the doorstep!'

The phone jangled in the still air, and Sunnu went to answer it. She was back five minutes later. 'That was Mr Vikram,' she said, looking meaningfully at Shiv.

Shiv rolled his eyes at Jody.

'You must keep out of his way, Shivam,' said his mother. 'Please try not to return to that place.'

Shiv looked as if he was about to protest, so Jody spoke up quickly. 'So long as we see some dolphins on the river tomorrow, I won't mind if we don't go back to that island, Shiv. And hey – we've got a six-hour return river trip. We're bound to see dolphins, aren't we?'

May 26 – just before bed – Sukhi Rest House
Only ten hours to go before we head up the river to
Mongla! I can't wait. It's going to be even more
interesting now that nearly everyone has decided to
come. Brittany was quite keen on the idea of a trip to
Mongla since she heard that we might see some tigers
from the safety of Dolphin Dreamer. *But then Ajay told*
her that tigers were very good swimmers. It took us
ages to calm her down.

There are so many exciting noises in the forest at
night. The sounds come straight into our bedroom,
because our window faces into the trees. You can hear
monkeys calling, and strange grunts that may be the
wild pigs they have around here. Brittany doesn't like
any of the noises. She says they are scary. It's just as
well she's fallen asleep already, because I've just heard
that tiger again, growling out in the forest. It sounded
even closer than it did this afternoon . . . Tigers can't
climb in through first-floor windows, can they?

Jody leant back from the *Dolphin Dreamer*'s deck
rails and closed her eyes. The cool morning breeze
in her hair felt wonderful.

They had left the Sukhi Rest House at seven that

morning, and had been chugging up the river for the last half an hour. Harry was deliberately taking *Dolphin Dreamer* slowly, to avoid making the carburetor problem any worse.

Jody turned round when Shiv tapped her on the shoulder.

'Your father has been showing us his website,' he said in excitement. 'I can't believe you can send all those pictures and stories to America.'

'It's amazing, isn't it?' Jody agreed. 'All my friends back in Florida log on to the website, to see where I am. Then they tell me in their emails how jealous they all are!'

Shiv peered over the side of the boat. 'Have you seen any dolphins yet?'

Almost in answer to his question, the water broke about fifty metres ahead of the boat, and the sleek grey back of a dolphin emerged.

'Mom, Dad!' Jody called. 'The dolphins are here!'

She watched closely as the water broke again. Was it an Irrawaddy? Could it even be the same one she and Shiv had seen the previous day, before they had met Mr Vikram?

'It's a Susu,' said Craig from behind her.

'Susie?' Jody echoed, confused. Since when did this dolphin have a name?

'No, not Susie!' Gina laughed, putting her arm round Jody's shoulders. 'A Susu. It's another name for a Ganges river dolphin. This one is female, I think – she's quite large. Ganges river dolphins can grow up to about two and a half metres long if they're female, but males only get to just over two metres.'

'Well, if she's female, we should call her Susie,' said Jody promptly.

Susie the dolphin breached again. This time Jody could see a long, toothed beak poking above the water.

'Why does she hold her beak above the water like that?' she asked in fascination.

'Ganges river dolphins come up to breathe at a very sharp angle,' Craig said. 'A very visible beak is the result. Ganges river dolphins are naturally quite sociable, too.'

Susie began a series of very fast clicks and whistles, nodding her strange, long beak in the air.

'She's definitely sociable,' said Jody. 'She's trying to talk to us!'

She leant over the railing to get a closer look. Susie immediately spun over on one side, and waved a flipper at Jody, who laughed and waved back.

'Actually, I think she's feeding,' smiled Gina. 'They use their flippers to sift through the mud on the riverbed, looking for food.'

With one final cheeky whistle, Susie slipped below the churning surface of the river, and was gone.

'She must have found something to eat,' said Jody.

Craig nodded. 'Maybe some tasty shrimps.'

'Glad you've seen a dolphin properly at last,' said Harry, stepping over to join them at the rail. Ravi and Sunnu followed him, talking quietly together. 'I've seen one or two from the *Dolphin Dreamer* these past couple of nights.'

'What else have you seen?' Jody asked.

'Crocodiles,' said Harry promptly. 'But you know that big one from the other day? Apparently the fishermen haven't seen her since that morning. Maybe she's found some other fishermen to steal from.'

Shiv looked surprised. 'I have never known Chalaka to miss a day's fishing,' he said.

Ravi and Sunnu also looked surprised, Jody thought. No, more than that – they looked *concerned*.

'When did the fishermen last see her?' Ravi asked.

'Like I told you,' said Harry. 'Yesterday morning, at the catch.'

Ravi and Sunnu exchanged a strange, silent glance. Jody was about to ask them what they were thinking, but her attention was caught by two or three birds – kingfishers, according to Dr Taylor – which flew like lightning across the river. And then she forgot all about it.

The sun was already quite high in the sky when *Dolphin Dreamer* reached the town of Mongla. It felt like a different country from the peace and quiet of the Sukhi Rest House. Hundreds of people were milling along the riverbank, browsing at the market stalls which had been set up along the water. Boats of all shapes and sizes had docked at the long bamboo jetty, and Jody could hear lively Indian music floating across the water.

'Mongla likes to enjoy itself on market day,' Ravi said to her as they all made their way up the jetty and into the town. 'Making music and making money – they go together very well, don't you think?'

Harry checked his watch. 'Cam and I'll make our way to the boatyard,' he said. 'Ravi, can you show us where to go?'

'I suggest we all meet back at the boat in two hours' time,' said Craig. 'It'll give you all a chance to explore.'

Mei Lin's eyes gleamed. 'I shall enjoy putting together a banquet fit for a king from this lot,' she laughed, indicating the market stalls. 'Brittany, can you help me? We will find some wonderful food, I am sure.'

Jody expected Brittany to say no. She didn't like chores at the best of times. But Brittany looked quite excited at the prospect of shopping at all the different stalls, and joined Mei Lin without a murmur.

'I don't envy the traders,' remarked Gina as Mei Lin and Brittany headed into the heart of the market. 'I think Mei Lin will drive a hard bargain!'

'Come on,' said Shiv, grabbing Jody's hand and pulling her into the market. 'Two hours isn't long for Mongla!'

Jody felt overwhelmed by the colour and energy of the town as Shiv dragged her from place to place. There were piles of exotic fruit, bales of brightly-coloured cotton and silk, squawking chickens and bleating goats everywhere. The air was warm and full of the smells of Sundarban life – animal and vegetable, burning incense and muddy river water. Jody peered into stalls where men were having their hair cut, eating bowls of steamed fish, even having their teeth looked at by a market dentist. She saw stalls with wicker cages of tiny singing birds, who filled the air with trilling and chirruping. She even saw a monkey stealing a banana from a market stall before chattering and disappearing down the street at speed, to the fury of the stallholder. Cheerful music pumped from every stall and every house along the way, and Jody lost all sense of time in the wonder of it all.

'Let's go and find Harry,' said Shiv at last. 'We must be back at the boat in a little while. Maybe he needs some help.'

They wandered down a side alley to the river, where they found a large open-sided building on the waterfront. Boats in various stages of repair lay

Busy Mongla market

in front of it on the riverbank, and the inside of the building was filled with sounds of hammering and banging.

Jody peered around, trying to catch sight of Harry. Two men were talking at the far end of the boatyard. One of the men looked familiar – but it wasn't Harry.

'It's Mr Vikram!' said Jody in surprise.

Shiv hissed through his teeth. 'He will probably shout at us again if he sees us,' he said. 'I think we should stay back here for now.'

They watched from a safe distance.

'He is talking to Khaled, the boatyard owner,' Shiv explained for Jody's benefit.

'Mr Vikram must be getting his boat fixed,' said Jody.

Shiv frowned. 'No, I think he is ordering a new boat. But maybe I heard wrong. Everyone knows Mr Vikram has no money – his shellfish business is not doing so well at the moment.'

They listened some more. Mr Vikram was waving his hands, and so was Khaled.

Shiv straightened up. 'It's probably nothing,' he shrugged. 'Harry's not here, so let's go back to *Dolphin Dreamer*. I don't know about you, but I'm hungry.'

* * *

'Good timing,' Gina greeted them as they made their way down the bamboo jetty and boarded *Dolphin Dreamer*. 'Mei Lin and Brittany have cooked up a feast, and we're about to tuck in. How was your morning?'

Before Jody had a chance to reply, Jimmy gave a shout and pointed down the jetty. They turned to see Dr Taylor staggering towards the boat, his arms absolutely full of fruit. A huge branch of papaya fruit hung over one shoulder, and a branch of bananas over the other. He was doing his best not to drop the twenty odd mangoes he was balancing in front of him.

'Wretched traders . . . wouldn't take no . . . for an answer,' he puffed, as he reached *Dolphin Dreamer*. 'I didn't . . . want it, but they kept piling it on. Where's . . . Mei Lin? Maybe she can do something useful with all this.'

He wobbled aboard and disappeared down into the galley.

'Well,' Gina remarked in amusement, 'thanks to Dr Taylor, it looks like we're going to be enjoying some local fruits for the rest of our stay!'

May 27 – lunchtime – on deck, Mongla jetty
Everyone had a great time in Mongla this morning! Mom
bought herself a gorgeous red and pink silk sari, and
Sunnu has promised to show her how to put it on. The
twins even got to see a snake charmer in the market.
Khaled the boatyard owner came round to Dolphin
Dreamer and fitted the new carburetor himself in half
an hour flat. The engine's now 'purring like a tiger', as
Harry fondly puts it.

On the subject of tigers, Brittany is sulking in her cabin
because the twins and Ajay sneaked up behind her in
the market and growled, making her scream and drop
a bag of chapati flour she and Mei Lin had just bought.
The bag burst and covered Brittany in flour from head
to foot! Needless to say, Brittany didn't see the funny
side, and she's still leaving a trail of flour whenever
she moves around.

Shiv and I never got round to mentioning Mr Vikram
and the boatyard. He was probably there for a perfectly
good reason, anyway. Must go, we're about to leave
and I want to make sure I get some of Dr Taylor's fruit
salad for dessert!

Jody forgot all about Mr Vikram on the way back to

the Sukhi Rest House. Susie the Ganges river dolphin bobbed up beside them again, and did her best to keep the boat entertained for most of the journey. She was joined by several others, all waving their long beaks in the air for what looked like the sheer fun of it. But there was still no sign of an Irrawaddy dolphin. Jody was beginning to feel a little pessimistic.

The Sukhi Rest House was just coming into view when there was a shout from the bow.

'Irrawaddy!'

Jody's heart leapt in her chest. Had she heard Shiv right, or were her ears playing tricks on her?

Shiv was beckoning her, grinning. 'Come over here, Jody!' he said. 'Quickly, or you'll miss it!'

Jody flew to the far side of the boat, narrowly beating her parents and the others to a prime position by the rails. They all stared out into the river.

All that could be seen of the Irrawaddy dolphin was its neat rounded head, as it sat up like a seal and stared at them out of the water. Jody saw immediately how different this species of dolphin was from Susie. It had a thick flexible neck, and it seemed to be cocking its head as it looked at them. It didn't have the same smile as a bottlenose dolphin. Instead, its mouth was set in a straight line, giving it an air of dignity and wisdom. Jody noticed a small scar above one eye, which almost made the dolphin look as if it was raising one eyebrow.

'It's very calm, isn't it?' Jody whispered to Shiv as she gazed into the small, deep-set eyes of the little dolphin. 'As if it knows the answer to world peace, or something.'

'Sandhi,' said Shiv.

Jody looked round at him, surprised. 'What does that mean?' she asked.

'S-A-N-D-H-I,' Shiv spelled it out. 'It is a Hindi word. It means peace.'

'I think that's what we should call her, then,' said Jody.

'How do you know it's a she?' Gina laughed.

Jody smiled. 'She just looks like a girl. Don't you think she's female?'

'More than likely,' Craig admitted. 'Judging from her size.'

Sandhi stared at them for a while longer, with the grave wisdom of an owl. Then she turned her head slightly and looked directly at Jody. Jody wished desperately that she was a bit nearer. 'Sandhi,' she whispered again.

At last, the dolphin sank below the water, and Jody was left staring at the calm surface of the river.

4

Jody opened her eyes in the darkness of the night. It felt very late – perhaps one or two o'clock in the morning. Something she couldn't quite place had brought her out of a deep sleep.

'Jody?' came Brittany's scared voice. 'Are you awake?'

Jody sat up and switched on the small bedside light.

Brittany was staring at her with large, frightened eyes. 'I can hear the tiger,' she whispered. 'It sounds really close.'

Jody heard a rumbling growl from the forest

outside the window. Her heart hammered in her chest, but she stayed calm. 'It's OK, Brittany,' she said. 'It's miles away. Go back to sleep.'

Brittany frowned uncertainly, then huddled down under her mosquito net. The tiger fell silent after a few more minutes. Soon Jody could hear Brittany breathing evenly, fast asleep again.

Jody switched off the light but lay awake for a while, listening to the noises of the night. Her mind was alert, and she didn't feel sleepy at all. The memory of Sandhi's serious dolphin face peeping out of the river earlier that day kept running through her head, making her smile. Where did the little Irrawaddy come from, she wondered? Why hadn't they seen her before, if she lived close to the rest house?

Jody decided that a drink of water might help her get back to sleep. She knew that the Kaushiks always kept a jug of iced water in the fridge, and so she climbed quietly out of bed and made her way down to the kitchen.

At the bottom of the stairs, she stopped and listened. She could hear voices – Sunnu and Ravi were talking in the living area. Jody felt puzzled. It was very late. What could they be talking about? From what she could hear, they sounded worried. Perhaps they were talking about the tiger?

She stood in the darkness for a moment, unsure about what to do. Then she walked into the kitchen, filled a glass with cold water, and headed back up to bed. Whatever Sunnu and Ravi were talking about, it was none of her business.

Jody got up early the next morning and wandered outside to the jetty. Philip Warner was painting, and he looked pleased to see her.

'What do you think?' he asked, indicating his painting. 'The sunrise was over pretty quickly, but I reckon I got most of it down on canvas.'

Jody settled down on the jetty beside him, and looked around at the swirling morning mist which cloaked the river. 'Weren't you worried about meeting the tiger face to face this morning?' she asked curiously. 'Haven't you heard that expression yet, the one about "Here the Tiger is always watching you"?'

Philip shrugged. 'You came out here, didn't you?'

'Yes,' Jody said slowly, 'but it was already light.

You must have been out here in the dark.'

'Well, between you and me, I wanted to see the tiger,' Philip told her. 'I like taking risks sometimes. It's just not the same, painting tigers from other people's photographs.'

'You're pretty interested in tigers, aren't you?' Jody commented.

'Of course,' Philip said. 'You can't help being interested in tigers in this area. There are so many stories about them. Many people believe that they are magical spirits – wicked magicians, warriors, gods! And because of this superstition, tiger bone and other parts are believed to have healing and strengthening powers in certain parts of the world. It makes them the most wonderful creatures to paint, knowing the myths that surround them.'

'What else do you paint?' Jody asked.

'Loggerhead turtles,' said Philip, ticking them off on his fingers. 'Crocodiles. Rhesus monkeys sometimes, and birds.'

'Do you ever paint dolphins?' Jody asked eagerly.

'It has been known,' said Philip, carefully putting his paints away in a battered leather case.

Before Jody could ask him any more questions,

Philip stood up. 'I'm going inside,' he said. 'Enjoy the rest of the dawn! But I have to say I'm dying for a cup of tea.'

May 28 – early morning – on the jetty of the Sukhi Rest House

The tiger growled away most of the night, and in between listening to it and thinking about Sandhi and Susie, my brain never got tired enough to go back to sleep. I thought I'd come out here and see if the fishermen were at work again, but I was too late – the sun had risen, and they'd brought in their catch already.

Philip Warner, the artist who's staying here, was sitting on the jetty beside Dolphin Dreamer *with his easel. He'd done a beautiful painting of the sunrise – bright slashes of pink and red. If I hadn't seen that amazing sunrise the other day, I would have thought he had made up the colours! Apparently he didn't sleep very well last night either. But his excuse was that he was too excited to sleep. He wanted to get outside and paint the tiger he could hear. I think he's only seen tigers from a distance, even though he's been here for over six months. It must be very frustrating, trying to paint an animal who doesn't like the attention!*

* * *

Jody closed her diary and headed back into the rest house. Gina looked up from her cup of coffee as Jody entered the kitchen. 'Morning,' she yawned. 'You and Philip are up early. Did you hear the tiger?'

'As if you could miss it,' said Jody, sitting down. 'Brittany woke up once, but then she slept like a stone through the rest of the night.' She looked curiously at her mother. 'Why are you up so early, Mom?' she asked.

Gina smiled. 'I need to update the Dolphin Universe website,' she said. 'Having seen that Irrawaddy yesterday, I now feel that I've got something to say. Web users haven't been logging on to hear about my new sari, or how comfortable the beds in the Sukhi Rest House are.'

'Did you get a picture?' asked Jody.

Gina shook her head. 'Stupidly, your dad and I left the camera here before we left for Mongla. I don't quite know what I'm going to do yet, but I'll think of something.'

Philip had been drinking his tea, standing quietly beside the kitchen sink. Suddenly he joined in the conversation. 'I have a picture you could use,' he said. 'Not a photo though, I'm afraid.'

Gina looked at him with interest. 'One of your paintings?' she asked.

'I have some sketches,' he said modestly. 'Just a few I've made recently. I'll show you, if you like. So long as your web users don't mind a bit of artistic licence?'

'How much licence?' Jody queried.

Philip laughed. 'I'm not into abstract art, if that's what you're wondering,' he said. 'Here, look.' He rummaged in the large bag he was carrying, and pulled out a sheaf of sketch paper, which he carefully spread out on the kitchen table.

Jody gasped. The pictures were beautiful. With a few bold pencil lines, Philip had captured several Irrawaddy dolphins perfectly. Their round heads, their solemn expressions, each dolphin had a separate and distinct character. One of the dolphins had a small scar above one eye. With mounting excitement, Jody felt sure that the picture was of Sandhi.

'These are wonderful, Philip,' said Gina, staring intently at the pictures. 'I'd love to use a couple. I think you may have just saved my life here. How much do we owe you?'

'Oh, I couldn't charge you,' said Philip, embarrassed. 'Just my name on the pictures will do.'

'We'll make sure we give you a glowing review on the Dolphin Universe page, then,' said Gina, smiling. 'Come on, let's go and scan these pictures in.'

The scanner and computer were still on board *Dolphin Dreamer*, so Jody, Gina and Philip made their way outside. The sun was rapidly burning off the morning mist, and the sky was getting brighter all the time.

'Philip,' said Jody, as Gina logged on to the website and powered up the scanner, 'where did you do those pictures? They are fantastic. I didn't know you could see so many Irrawaddies in one place.'

Philip looked pleased. 'A little place I've found upriver,' he said. 'I don't think anyone else knows about it. A family of Irrawaddies lives there. I've been going there for a couple of months now. They used to disappear at the first sight of me, but they gradually got used to me. Now they genuinely don't seem to notice when I arrive.'

'Can I ask where this place is?' asked Gina. 'You see, Craig and I really need to collect some data on the Irrawaddy. We haven't had much luck so far. This family would be perfect research material for us.'

Philip looked thoughtful. 'I haven't taken anyone there before,' he said. 'Not even Shiv knows about it. I'm not sure the dolphins would appreciate a larger audience.'

'I understand your concern, Philip,' Gina nodded. 'But I can't tell you how important our research is. The Irrawaddy's natural habitat is constantly under threat from development and pollution, and numbers are dwindling. We really don't know very much about this little dolphin, and it needs all the help it can get.'

Philip was silent for a minute or two. 'All right,' he said eventually. 'I can see that it is important. And I hardly need to tell a dolphin expert about the need to respect these animals. I'll take you there later on, if you like.'

Jody couldn't hold it in any longer. 'Please can I come too?' she begged. 'I . . .'

She stopped. She couldn't put her finger on why it was so important to see the dolphins, and perhaps to see Sandhi again. She just knew with all her heart that all she wanted in the world was to see the Irrawaddy family in their secret home.

Philip shook his head. 'I really don't think taking all three of you is a good idea,' he said. 'I'm sorry, Jody. We might drive them away from their home, and I'd hate to be responsible for that.'

Jody's shoulders sagged. She could see Philip's point, and respected him for making it. But it was very hard to hear.

Gina was looking thoughtful. 'Jody is very good with dolphins, Philip,' she said. 'She's spent pretty much her whole life learning about them and living with them. I have a suggestion, which I hope you will consider.'

Jody looked hopefully at her mother.

'How about if I drop out, and Jody takes my place?' Gina suggested.

'But Mom, your research!' Jody gasped.

Gina smiled. 'Philip, do you think I could go some other time?' she asked. 'Craig can make notes on his own. I'd love to see the dolphins, but I think Jody might burst with frustration if we don't let her go. And she's got the makings of a great marine observer. What do you think?'

May 28 – afternoon – somewhere on cloud nine
I have the best mother in the world. I couldn't believe
it when Philip agreed to take me to see the Irrawaddies
instead of Mom. Dad was happy to have me along, so
it's been decided. We're going after lunch. I've never
felt less like lunch in my life! I keep staring at my watch,
wishing the hands would move faster. I might see
Sandhi again this afternoon – up close!

'All set?' said Philip, grinning at Jody and her dad from
behind the controls of the Kaushiks' small red launch.

Craig checked that he had everything he needed
– camera, notepad, pen. 'As ready as I'll ever be!'
he smiled, climbing into the launch.

Jody jumped aboard behind him. She had her
camera with her, and her diary. She knew they might
end up waiting some time to see the dolphins, so
she planned to describe every last detail of the secret
bay in her journal.

The boat's engine gave a throaty roar, and Philip
pulled away from the jetty. Soon they were speeding
down the river, cutting through the breakers with
ease. It was a good, powerful boat – unlike Shiv's
little dinghy.

Philip took them off the main course of the river after about fifteen minutes. Soon, the boat was cruising down smaller water channels, beneath a canopy of tall, dark mangrove trees. Left, right, left. He seemed to know his way very well.

At last, the launch drew up in a calm, leafy inlet. Philip moored the boat, and motioned to Jody and Craig to step ashore. The island was quiet and serene, dappled with pale light filtering down through the trees.

Philip pointed to a shaded water channel just to the left of a huge, gnarled tree. 'The family bases itself here,' he whispered, deftly setting up his painting stool and flipping open his sketchpad. 'They aren't home yet, but they never stray very far. I expect they'll be along within the next hour or so. Are you OK waiting?'

Jody settled down beside the water. Her dad pulled out his notebook and camera, and started jotting a few notes.

They waited for a while. In that time, Jody noticed all kinds of things about the Irrawaddies' inlet. Tiny red crabs appeared in the shoreline mud, waving bright red claws at the sky. Rope-like lianas hung

Our patience is rewarded . . .

from the trees above them, thick and heavy. The brilliant flash of a butterfly caught Jody's eye, and she heard the distant chatter of a monkey somewhere up in the trees. She made a few notes in her diary, and sketched some small dolphins in the margin.

At last, their patience was rewarded. Jody held her breath as three sleek grey bodies coasted silently into the inlet. One of the Irrawaddies promptly sank from view at the sight of visitors, but the other two seemed unconcerned.

Jody immediately recognized the smaller of the two remaining dolphins. She'd know that face with its quizzical scar anywhere. Sandhi looked at her, tilting her rounded head just like a dog. Jody stared back happily.

Sandhi clicked rapidly at Jody, as if she was trying to communicate something. Then she flicked her tail and sank a few inches below the water, until only her head was showing, still watching Jody with interest.

The third dolphin returned after about ten minutes, apparently having decided that Jody and her father were harmless. Sandhi and her family stayed for another twenty minutes, feeding quietly along the riverbank. Jody thought of the little red crabs she'd seen earlier. They were obviously the Irrawaddies' favourite food.

Before long, the small family of dolphins turned on an unspoken command and headed back out to the river.

'I think that's it,' said Philip regretfully, folding up his sketchpad. 'Not long today, I'm afraid.'

'It was a great start,' said Craig with a smile. He capped his pen. 'What beautiful animals. I got some lovely pictures. Thank you so much for bringing us, Philip.'

Jody climbed into the launch, and stared back over her shoulder as Philip pulled away from the shore. She hoped that Philip would bring her back some day soon. She felt her father's hand on her shoulder, and looked round. Philip was pointing at something on the far shore.

Jody wasn't certain, but she thought she caught a glimpse of a yellow and black striped face, peering out at them from the undergrowth. Her whole body tensed. Was it a tiger? But within a moment, the face had gone.

5

May 29 – evening – Sukhi Rest House
You wouldn't believe how much rain has fallen in the
last twenty-four hours. I was quite relieved to wake up
this morning and find that the rest house was still
standing on the riverbank, not floating downstream. I
had no idea that rain could be so noisy! It's been
throwing it down all day, and it's pretty impressive to
watch. The whole sky looks like a waterfall, and the
river has been whipped up into a frothy, chocolatey
swirl. Somehow, I don't think the fishermen went out
this morning. Even Harry and Cam have been driven
off Dolphin Dreamer, and have been inside all day.

'I'm so *bored*,' Brittany moaned, staring out of the window. The rain was still steadily falling.

'But you've won the last five games!' objected Harry, staring down at the pack of cards he was holding in his hands. 'How can you be bored?'

Jody put her cards down with a sigh. They had been playing most of the afternoon, and even she had to admit that it was getting pretty dull. She wondered how Sandhi and her family were doing. Did river dolphins suffer in bad weather like this? After all, they couldn't dive deep to escape the rain like sea dolphins.

'I hope it isn't the moonsoon already,' said Ravi.

'So do I!' said Harry fervently. 'After all that business with the carburetor, it would be really bad luck if the monsoon came early.'

'We could be here for months,' sighed Jimmy. 'And we've played with all of Ajay's toys already.'

Sunnu leant over and whispered something to Ravi, who immediately frowned.

'Is something the matter?' asked Gina.

'I'm a little concerned . . .' said Sunnu, and then stopped.

'Concerned about what?' asked Jody, intrigued.

She suddenly remembered the hushed conversation she'd overheard a couple of nights earlier. 'Concerned about the tiger again?'

Craig snorted. 'I think the tiger's probably too wet and miserable to be worrying about us,' he said.

'No, not the tiger,' said Sunnu slowly. 'We think the tiger has left. We haven't heard it for a few days.' She glanced at Ravi. 'I'm just concerned about the roof,' she said at last. 'With all this rain, I think we may have a leak.'

'I'll look at it for you tonight, Sunnu,' Philip offered, looking up from his sketchpad. Jody was amused to see that he had been drawing her brothers and Ajay. He'd captured their bored faces perfectly.

'Thank you, Philip,' said Sunnu, 'but it really won't be necessary. Ravi has mended leaks in this roof before. It is very easy.' She stood up. 'Now I must prepare some supper for you. Please excuse me.'

She walked into the kitchen. After a few moments, Ravi followed her. Jody was left with the strange feeling that they were still uneasy about something. And it wasn't the roof.

* * *

After supper, everyone made their excuses and went to bed early. There really was nothing else to do.

Brittany checked her bed suspiciously. 'I bet the rain'll leak right on to my head in the night,' she complained. 'That would be typical.'

Jody scrambled into bed and pulled the duvet up. 'Brittany, do you think everything's OK with Ravi and Sunnu?' she asked.

Brittany looked surprised. 'Apart from the leaking roof, you mean?' she queried. 'Why wouldn't everything be OK?'

Jody shrugged. 'I've just got a funny feeling,' she said.

'So have I,' Brittany grumbled, climbing into bed. 'I've got a funny feeling about this leak. If I scream in the night, you'll know it's either the tiger or the leak that's got me.' She suddenly grinned. 'Maybe Philip would come and rescue me,' she said coyly. 'Don't you think he's gorgeous? Maybe it's worth screaming in the night just in case! Night, Jody.'

Jody said goodnight and lay back in the dark, letting the sound of the drumming rain soothe her to sleep.

* * *

Brilliant sunshine was pouring into the bedroom when Jody opened her eyes the next morning. She jumped out of bed and ran to the window.

The Sundarbans looked magical. The leaves on the trees gleamed and shone in the sun. Wisps of steam rose from the wet, black trunks of the mangrove trees. The sky was a bright, glorious blue, and there wasn't a cloud in the sky. It was like a different place.

Brittany sat up in bed and yawned. 'Sun at last!' she said sleepily. 'About time.'

Jody quickly dragged on her clothes and ran downstairs. Both her parents and Philip were already up, and sitting around the table.

'It seems our fears about the monsoon were premature,' said Gina with a smile, looking up as Jody came in. 'Your father and I are going to take a look at the Ganges dolphins today, Jody. Would you like to join us? Apparently several families live about half an hour's walk downriver.'

She looked across at Philip. 'Alternatively,' she said, 'Philip is planning to head back to the Irrawaddy inlet for some more sketching. He says you were a pleasure to have along yesterday, and he wouldn't mind some more company today.

Maybe you'd prefer to go back there?'

'What a choice!' Jody joked, helping herself to a bowl of cereal. 'I'd love to see some more Ganges dolphins again, Mom, but . . .'

'You've lost your heart to the Irrawaddies,' Craig finished her sentence for her.

Jody flashed an apologetic smile at her parents. 'You know me pretty well, don't you, Dad?' she said with a grin.

Normally, Jody would have jumped at the chance of spending the day with her parents to help them observe the Ganges river dolphins. But what her dad had said was true. There was something about the Irrawaddies, and Sandhi in particular, which had captured her imagination. She couldn't wait to see them again.

'That's fine,' said Philip. 'I think we may need to bring Shiv along as well, as all the rain has made the river a little trickier to navigate than the other day.'

Brittany appeared in the kitchen. Jody noticed with interest that she'd applied a touch of make-up this morning, and had taken particular care with her clothes.

'Morning, everyone,' she said casually. She

glanced across at Philip under her eyelashes. 'Morning, Philip,' she added, a blush creeping up her neck.

'And a gorgeous morning it is, too,' said Philip, raising his mug of tea towards her.

Brittany blushed a little more, and busied herself with cutting up a fresh mango.

Jody caught her mother's eye and tried not to laugh. It was so obvious that Brittany had a crush on Philip!

'So, what's everyone doing today?' Brittany asked, looking across at Philip again.

'This and that,' said Craig.

'What about you, Philip?' Brittany looked hopefully across at the tall English artist.

'Jody and I are off sketching and admiring Irrawaddies,' said Philip. 'Shiv's coming too, to help us navigate.'

Brittany flicked her hair back from her face. 'I love Irrabodies,' she said earnestly. 'Could I maybe come too?'

'Are you any good at keeping quiet?' Philip asked, stirring his tea.

Jody managed to turn a laugh into a cough.

Brittany glared at her. 'Oh, yes,' she said, turning back to Philip. 'So – could I come?'

'I don't see why not,' Philip said after a moment. 'The dolphins seemed fine with two new visitors the other day. I think we might be able to risk three today. But we'll be leaving in about ten minutes. Think you'll be ready in time?'

Brittany had a mouthful of mango. She tried to nod eagerly, but somehow managed to choke and cough the mango back on to her plate. Blushing fierily, she excused herself from the table, and fled up to the bedroom.

Poor Philip, thought Jody with a grin. What had he let himself in for?

Twenty minutes later, Shiv eased the Kaushiks' launch away from the jetty. The water was wild and frothy, and it was a struggle to get into the calmer water in the centre of the river. Brittany shrieked and clutched Philip's arm – quite unnecessarily, Jody thought, as she helped Shiv to hold the tiller still.

The sun blazed down on the water, which glared fiercely in the light. Through the rushing sound of the river, Jody could hear the steady drip-drip-drip of rain from the trees along the bank. It was as if the rainstorm had washed the whole of the Sundarbans clean.

'Are you sure it's this way?' said Jody, looking at the river with confusion. There were more channels than she remembered, and the river seemed much wider.

'Yes,' said Philip, pointing at an enormous mangrove tree up ahead. 'I always head for that tree over there. Then it's about another five minutes further along, to the left.'

Shiv obediently followed Philip's instructions, and the boat struggled along through the current. The river boiled around them, flinging up waves and wetting them every now and again. Brittany's hair was looking frizzier by the minute, despite her surreptitious attempts to keep it smooth and close to her head. Jody tried not to think about the crocodiles, which she knew would happily gobble them all up if the boat overturned.

At last, Shiv drew the boat into the familiar inlet. The mossy green shore seemed smaller than it had before – the water levels had risen considerably in the night.

Brittany scrambled out of the boat. 'So what do we do now?' she asked loudly.

'Shhh,' said Philip, Jody and Shiv immediately.

'Oops,' Brittany whispered. 'Sorry. So, what do we do?'

'We wait and see—' Philip began to say.

Jody touched his sleeve and pointed. The Irrawaddies were already skulling gently in the shallow water channel and feeding along the riverbed.

'I think they have been here for some time,' Shiv whispered, settling down on the bank. 'The storm has not disturbed the water here so much. They have been sheltering, I think.'

Jody recognized Sandhi again with a rush of delight. The dolphin seemed pleased to see her – she kept her head boldly above the water and clicked softly in welcome. In the shallow inlet, Jody could see her more clearly. She had a stout middle, short powerful flippers and a small dorsal fin on her back.

The other two dolphins still kept their distance, although Jody could see their markings this time. She guessed they were both male. The bigger one had a nick in his dorsal fin, and the other had a mottled marking on his flank.

'They're cute,' said Brittany, sounding as if she didn't really care. She yawned and checked her watch. 'How long are we staying?'

'Just until I get that smaller male down on paper,' said Philip, busily sketching. 'He's pretty elusive. This is the first time he's stayed still long enough for me to draw him.'

Brittany moved closer to the water. 'Hey, this one's letting me get really close!' she said, forgetting to keep her voice down. 'I think he likes me!'

The big male lay stock still in the water, watching Brittany with beady black eyes as she approached. Suddenly the dolphin's muscular back flexed, and he squirted her sharply with a jet of water.

'Hey!' Brittany jumped up with a bellow.

The others burst out laughing. Even the dolphins, who had retreated from the shore, seemed to be grinning.

'He didn't like you so close!' spluttered Shiv.

'That was amazing!' said Jody. 'I've never seen a dolphin spit water like that before.'

'Well, I hope I never see it again,' said Brittany furiously, mopping herself up. 'Now look at me!'

Brittany gets a surprise!

There was a sudden crashing sound in the undergrowth. Something was approaching them fast.

'What's that noise?' Brittany quavered, looking fearfully into the dark green forest.

'Quick,' said Shiv instantly. 'Into the boat!'

He hustled them towards the launch, looking over his shoulder the whole time. The rustling was getting louder. Jody's stomach lurched. What if it was a tiger?

'What—' she began, as she jumped into the boat, pulling Brittany in after her.

'No time to argue!' Shiv insisted, pushing Philip into the boat and leaping in behind him. 'It's a boar!'

An ugly-looking wild pig shot out of the undergrowth, snorting furiously. Its legs pounded like pistons, and it cut a huge swathe through the grass and bamboo. Brittany shrieked. In a few whirlwind seconds, the boar disappeared again, ploughing a long, pale furrow through the jungle and out of sight. A line of small, heavy hoofprints showed that it had charged straight across the area where they had all been sitting only moments before.

'Well,' said Shiv after a moment of silence. 'He was in a hurry.' He looked very serious for a moment. 'I think maybe the tiger was after him.'

Brittany looked even more panic-stricken. 'I don't want to be eaten by a t . . . tiger!' she wailed.

Jody tried to breathe normally, but her chest felt as if it was about to explode. Her legs felt loose and wobbly, like two bits of string. Boars didn't get out of the way for just anybody. She'd seen the animal's sharp tusks, and the way they cut through the grass like butter.

'Is everyone OK?' asked Philip.

Brittany let out a sob, and he put his arm round her. Jody looked across the bow of the boat to the Irrawaddy inlet. She wasn't surprised to see that the dolphins had disappeared.

'I think we should stay in the boat for a few more minutes,' Shiv suggested. 'Then we can go back. The boar won't return. And it wasn't really being chased by a tiger, Brittany,' he added, looking slightly shamefaced. 'I was only joking. Boars do that all the time.'

'Some joke,' Brittany sniffed, and huddled up to Philip again.

'The dolphins may not come back today,' said Philip, 'but I'd like to wait a little longer, just in case.'

Jody looked back at the path the boar had carved through the forest. It looked like a neat, inviting tunnel. 'I'd like to check that out,' she said suddenly, pointing at the tunnel. 'See where it goes. Do you think it's safe, Shiv?'

Shiv smiled. 'We will wait a little while, just to make sure the boar has gone,' he said. 'Then we can go, if we are careful. Maybe we'll find some more animals I can tell you about.'

'I'll stay with Philip,' said Brittany immediately.

They waited a further ten minutes, just to make sure that the boar wasn't coming back. Then, cautiously, they climbed ashore again.

'We'll be back in a quarter of an hour,' Jody promised, as she and Shiv headed down the boar's path.

'OK,' said Philip, settling down beside the water again with Brittany beside him. 'No rush.'

Picking her way through the grass, following Shiv into the forest, Jody felt a frisson of fear. The forest was such a strange place. Maybe this wasn't such a good idea. But somehow, she knew she was safe with Shiv. She trusted him not to let them come to any harm.

The forest grew darker. The boar's path ploughed ahead of them, straight as an arrow. Jody looked up. The tops of the trees disappeared above her, straight and tall. Birds screeched among the leaves, and she heard quiet rustling in the grasses and roots at her feet. The forest had a magical quality about it. Jody felt she could walk for ever, and never reach the end.

'Hey!' Shiv exclaimed, bringing Jody up short where the boar's path ended at a deep water channel. 'Look at that!'

Jody looked, but didn't quite believe what her eyes were telling her. If the boar hadn't ripped away part of the undergrowth, they would never have seen it. A gleaming speedboat was lying in front of them, bobbing gently in the water.

6

'What a beautiful boat,' Jody remarked, staring at it. She couldn't help wondering why someone would leave it lying around in the middle of the forest. It didn't look like the sort of boat the fishermen used, but they hadn't seen any tourists around.

'Yes, it is beautiful,' Shiv agreed with a frown. 'But why is it here?'

The smell of fresh paint wafted up to them. The boat was sleek and fast-looking. It had no name, just a serial number painted on its side. A canvas tarpaulin covered the open seats. Jody pulled it back, and sniffed at the combination of fresh engine oil and new leather seats. Nothing had been left in the boat. It looked as if it had never been used. But if that was true, what was it doing here, in the middle of nowhere?

Jody looked around, but there was no sign of anyone. It was just her and Shiv, standing in the dappled green silence of the mangrove trees.

'I think we should show Philip,' said Shiv, looking at her.

Without waiting for Jody's reply, he turned around and started back towards Philip and Brittany. Jody hurried after him, her head full of questions.

'That was quick,' said Philip, looking up from his sketchpad as they burst out of the undergrowth.

Jody noticed immediately that Sandhi and her family had returned. They were skulling gently in the shallows and feeding along the bottom of the river again, as if the boar had never been there.

'We found something strange,' Shiv blurted out.

Brittany looked scared. 'The boar wasn't heading back this way, was he?'

'We found a boat, hidden in the undergrowth,' said Jody. 'We think you should see it, too.'

Philip stood up. 'A boat?' he echoed curiously. 'But no one ever comes here! I should know, I've been here often enough. Where is it?'

Shiv led the way back down the boar's tunnel. Jody was next, followed closely by Philip and Brittany. This time, Jody didn't notice the light, or the silence, or the animal noises that were coming from every side.

Brittany, on the other hand, did. 'It's pretty dark in here,' she said anxiously. 'Are you sure this is OK?' She shrieked as a monkey above her gave a loud scream, which echoed around the trees.

'It's just a little further,' said Jody over her shoulder.

'But what if there are snakes?' Brittany whimpered.

Philip reached out and took her hand. 'No snakes are going to get you,' he said reassuringly.

Brittany blushed. Then she gave a wobbly smile, and fell silent. Jody decided that Philip was a very useful influence on Brittany's theatrical nerves.

Shiv came to an abrupt stop at the end of the path. 'There,' he said, pointing.

The boat was still bobbing gently in the water channel in front of them.

Philip whistled. 'That's some machine,' he said admiringly. 'But what on earth is it doing here?'

'That's what we want to know,' Jody agreed, frowning.

The river was just as swollen and full on the way back. But this time, Shiv was taking the Kaushiks' launch with the flow of the water. It flew along like an arrow, sometimes dangerously fast, spinning and swirling on the changing currents. Shiv had a difficult time controlling the tiller, even with Jody's help. They all got soaked, and narrowly avoided crashing into the shore once or twice.

At last, Shiv pulled the launch safely out of the fast-running currents in the middle of the river, and guided it into the Sukhi Rest House jetty.

Harry Pierce had been watching them approach from the deck of *Dolphin Dreamer*. Jody noticed that he and Cameron had lashed down the sails as tightly as they would go. Harry clearly wasn't taking any chances with the weather.

When they got close to the jetty, Harry jumped off *Dolphin Dreamer* and strode towards them, beckoning for the rope. Shiv lobbed it upwards. It went whistling towards Harry with perfect accuracy.

'You're a handy sailor, Shiv,' Harry said admiringly, lashing the rope firmly to the jetty. 'That looked like a tough trip.'

Tough was an understatement, Jody thought. She'd never been so pleased to see solid ground in her life.

'More of a rollercoaster ride,' Brittany joked nervously, climbing on to the jetty.

Philip passed his bag and his stool up to Brittany, and climbed out of the boat as well. 'I have to say, I've enjoyed rollercoaster rides more,' he confessed. 'You know that they don't have crocodiles waiting for you if you fall out!'

'Come on,' Shiv said urgently, scrambling on to the jetty. 'Let's go and tell the others about that boat we found. My parents will want to know.'

'Careful!' Jody called after him, as he ran towards the rest house. 'The jetty is very slippery— oh!'

She watched in horror as Shiv suddenly lost his footing in a smooth, shining puddle of water. He skidded sharply, flew up in the air and then landed on the deck with a sickening crunch. He lay ominously still.

Shiv takes a tumble!

'Shiv!' screamed Brittany, rushing up to him. 'Are you OK?'

'Philip, go and get the Kaushiks,' said Harry urgently, running down the jetty.

'Right away,' Philip said and sprinted towards the house calling for Sunnu and Ravi.

Jody flew towards her friend, her heart hammering in her chest. To her enormous relief, Shiv groaned and opened his eyes.

'My ankle . . . hurts,' he said through gritted teeth.

Jody could see that his left ankle was already swelling up.

'Just lie still,' said Harry. 'Your parents will be out in a minute.'

The Kaushiks ran out on the deck, followed closely by Philip and the McGraths.

'Whatever happened?' Gina exclaimed.

'Shiv ran and slipped,' Jody explained, pointing at the offending puddle.

Jimmy and Sean peered down at Shiv, who was lying on his back and groaning quietly. 'Cool,' said Jimmy, impressed. 'Look, his ankle's like a balloon. Do you think maybe it's broken?'

'Did it go snap?' Sean asked Brittany.

Brittany was taking off her jacket to put under Shiv's head. 'What a disgusting question,' she complained.

Ajay pushed forward. 'That's nothing,' he said. 'I broke both my ankles once.'

'Not at the same time, Ajay,' said Ravi wryly.

Sunnu felt Shiv's ankle, and Shiv moaned with pain. 'I don't think it's broken,' she said at last.

'Shouldn't we get a doctor?' Craig asked with concern.

'The nearest doctor is fifty miles away,' said Ravi.
'We only call him in an emergency. Sunnu has a
medicine box. We will have him as good as new
before you know it.'

Sunnu gently strapped up Shiv's ankle with a
bandage she had brought out of the house. Then
Philip and Craig helped him to his feet.

'I think we shall put you to bed and give you
something to help you sleep,' said Sunnu, stroking
Shiv's forehead gently. 'Sleep is the best thing.'

Philip lifted Shiv up and carried him into the
house. It must hurt a lot if Shiv isn't complaining
about going to bed, Jody thought. She knew that he
hated sitting still or sleeping any longer than he
had to.

Philip and Craig helped Shiv up to bed.

'Come with me, Jody.' Sunnu beckoned her into
the kitchen.

Jody followed and watched as Sunnu set to work
in the kitchen, pulling leaves and seeds out of a small
box she kept by the sink. Sunnu pounded them
together with a handful of cornmeal and a splash of
water. The result was a gluey brown paste, with a
sharp antiseptic smell.

'What are you going to do with that?' Jody asked.

'I'll put this on his ankle,' Sunnu said. 'It will help the healing.'

'But what is it?' Jody wanted to know.

Sunnu smiled. 'A forest remedy,' she said. 'The Sundarbans is like a giant medicine box, if you know where to look for plants.' She rinsed out the bowl, and took a handful of different leaves. She pounded them together, as she had with the poultice for Shiv's ankle. Only this time, she added hot water and sugar and poured the concoction into a mug.

'Here,' she said, handing the mug to Jody. 'Can you take it up to Shivam? He will be glad of it.'

Jody sniffed it. A warm, lemony scent rose from the mug. It smelled nice, and Jody hoped it would work. It was certainly very different from any of the pills her doctor prescribed for her back home!

Shiv had taken three sips before falling asleep, his forehead less creased with pain now. As she came slowly back downstairs, Jody was filled with a new respect for the Sundarbans, its magical plants and the wisdom of its people.

She yawned hard as she walked into the kitchen.

Although it was barely four o'clock, she felt exhausted. It had been a very long day.

'Come and sit down,' said Gina, patting the stool next to her in the kitchen. 'You look shattered. Did those Irrawaddy dolphins give you the runaround today?'

Jody sank down next to her mother. 'No, they were lovely,' she said. 'But then a boar came and we had to jump into the boat—'

Suddenly she remembered the boat in the inlet. With all the excitement about Shiv, it had totally gone out of her head. Quickly, she told the others.

'A speedboat?' exclaimed Ravi, leaning forward at the table. 'Are you sure?'

'It was brand new, and we think someone had hidden it,' said Jody. 'If the boar hadn't run through the undergrowth, we would never have seen it.'

'This is serious,' said Ravi. There was a new heaviness in his voice. 'It means that our suspicions may be right.' He glanced at Sunnu.

'What suspicions?' Craig asked with surprise.

'Poachers,' said Sunnu quietly.

There was a sudden shocked silence.

'Ravi and I have believed for some time that

something was wrong in the forest,' Sunnu continued. 'We heard stories of animals disappearing.'

'That old crocodile!' said Brittany suddenly.

Sunnu nodded. 'Also some turtles, a week before you came. We heard about them on the UNESCO radio band. Marine turtles are rare, and UNESCO watches them closely. And we are now wondering about the tiger we have heard lately. All of a sudden, it has gone very quiet.'

'That's why you appeared so worried the other day!' Jody exclaimed, putting two and two together as she recalled the voices she had overheard in the night, and the strange conversation about the leaking roof.

Ravi nodded apologetically. 'We didn't want to worry you, until we had some kind of proof. The leaking roof was also a concern, but it is true – the poachers were worrying us more.'

'This is not the first time, I'm afraid,' sighed Sunnu. 'They came six months ago.' She looked at Jody. 'You know the Irrawaddy dolphin family you have been visiting? There are only three of them, yes?'

Jody nodded with dread in her heart.

'Six months ago, there were five,' said Sunnu simply.

Jody gasped. Sandhi had lost two members of her family to poachers? It didn't seem possible. 'But why do the poachers want Irrawaddy dolphins?' she asked. 'They're hardly ever kept in captivity. They aren't natural performers. Surely poachers would take bottlenoses, or other more sociable dolphins? I don't understand.'

Gina took Jody's hand. 'They are not taken for zoos, Jody,' she said, as gently as she could.

'Your mother is right,' Ravi said. 'There is a rich trade in the Far East for dolphin meat and oil. Places like China and Japan. The meat is smuggled over the borders. The smugglers bribe the customs officers, and it is hushed up. It is an ugly business.'

It took a moment for Ravi's words to sink in. Jody put her hand to her mouth. She felt sick.

'Tiger bone, too,' Ravi continued. 'And crocodiles and turtles. It is said that these animals have powerful spirits, and if you use them in medicines, they can work miracles.'

Jody remembered the conversation she had had with Philip on the jetty a couple of days earlier, about

94

tigers and their magical qualities. Hearing about the poachers gave Philip's stories a sinister meaning.

'But that's not true!' Jody burst out.

'We know,' said Sunnu sadly. 'Also, I think the poachers know. But they can make a lot of money this way, and so they do not care.'

Visions of Sandhi and the rest of her family being taken by the poachers filled Jody's mind. 'We have to stop them,' she said passionately. 'Before they kill any more animals. Now that we've found their boat, surely we can stop them?'

'We don't know for sure that the boat belongs to the poachers,' Philip pointed out.

'But we can start enquiring, can't we Ravi?' said Craig.

Ravi nodded. 'We will also tell the UNESCO officials. They are very worried about preserving the forest from men like these poachers, and they have special means to help us – boats, and trained men. They work closely with the police too.' He looked very solemn. 'If we are right, and the poachers are back, we will need all the help we can get.'

Something was niggling in Jody's mind –

something about a new boat. She had a feeling it might be very important. 'I want to go back to the inlet,' she said, standing up abruptly from the table. 'I think maybe I know something about the boat.'

The others looked at her in surprise.

'Maybe?' said Brittany, raising her eyebrows.

'That's the thing,' said Jody, irritated with herself. 'I can't remember exactly what. If I see the boat again, maybe I'll remember.'

And maybe I won't, she thought unhappily. *But I've got to try.*

7

Craig checked his watch. 'We have enough time before the light begins to fail,' he said. 'And the river looks calmer. Jody, do you really think returning to the inlet will help you to remember something useful?'

'I'm not sure, Dad,' Jody confessed. 'But I think we should go anyway. I want to see if the dolphins are OK.' This was her biggest fear – that Sandhi and her family might be spirited away by the poachers before they returned.

'I haven't seen these dolphins yet,' said Gina, standing up from the table. 'I'll come with you.

Ravi, Sunnu – do you want to join us?'

Ravi shook his head. 'I have to stay here,' he said. 'I will make some phone calls, and start asking about the boat. I will also contact UNESCO.'

'I must stay for Shiv,' said Sunnu, 'and the other children, too. Also, your friends aren't back from their trip yet. I should be here when they return.'

Dr Taylor, Maddie, Cam and Mei Lin had gone on a tour that morning, travelling with a group of honey collectors deep into the forest. The collectors only worked in April and May, and they covered parts of the Sundarbans which very few people had ever seen.

Ravi frowned. 'The river is very difficult to navigate after the heavy rain,' he said. 'The waters are a little calmer now, but I am concerned that you may have difficulty reaching the inlet again.'

'I'll go with them,' Philip offered immediately. 'I've been taking the boat there for several months, and I know the route. And after Shiv's help this morning, I think I know what to do now that the river is so high.'

'I don't want to go again,' said Brittany decisively. 'That boat ride today made me feel sick. I can get rides like that in fairgrounds back home.'

'That's good,' Sunnu smiled. 'You can help me to prepare the supper, and keep an eye on Shivam and the other children.'

Sean, Jimmy and Ajay were tumbling around the living area, laughing and joking. Little Ambika was watching them with wide dark eyes.

'We'll be back as soon as we can,' Craig promised the Kaushiks. 'And hopefully, Jody will have remembered something useful about this mysterious boat. We'll do everything in our power to help you stop these poachers, don't worry.'

The Kaushiks still looked anxious as they waved Jody, her parents and Philip off at the jetty. And with good reason – the river was still high, and whirled around the boat as Philip steered them back up the river.

Fortunately, the river seemed a little easier to navigate this time. The waters were beginning to calm down again after the rain, and they reached the inlet after less than half an hour.

Jody jumped ashore and lashed the boat to the mangrove tree stump, as before. She ran to the far side of the island – but the water channel was silent and empty.

'They aren't here,' she said, as her parents joined her at the water's edge. 'I hope . . .' She left the sentence unfinished. She knew her parents understood her perfectly.

'I'm sure they're safe, Jody,' Craig said gently. 'After all, you've been here before when they've not been around. And they'll be even safer once we've sorted out the mystery with this boat. Now, where is it?'

The boar's trail was still clearly marked as Jody led her parents through the forest. They found the boat again within five minutes. Craig looked it over carefully, peering under the tarpaulin and running his hand along the sleek, painted hull.

'Well?' Gina prompted, looking hopefully at Jody. 'Does it ring any bells, now that you can see it again?'

Jody stood and stared at the boat. Images swam up inside her mind – a conversation she had heard recently. But the details stayed firmly out of reach. 'I'm sorry,' she said with frustration. 'Nothing.'

Chewing her lip, she followed her parents back down the boar's trail, looking back over her shoulder a couple of times. But the boat was keeping its secret locked up tight.

'The dolphins are back!'

Philip's exclamation brought Jody speedily back to reality. She ran eagerly over to the water's edge with her parents.

'Two males!' Gina said with satisfaction. 'Aren't they beautiful?'

Only two? Jody looked. Sure enough, the mottled male and the big one which had spat water at Brittany were clearly visible in the shallow water. Where was the female? Where was Sandhi?

'Sandhi's missing,' she burst out, falling to her knees and looking desperately up and down the water channel. 'The female, the one I've been watching.'

Gina and Craig looked at each other with concern.

'Does she always stay with the males?' Craig asked.

Jody tried to think. 'The first time we saw her, in the river, she was alone,' she said. 'But every time we've been to the inlet, they have been together.'

'It's true,' Philip agreed, looking concerned. 'We either have all three of them here, or none at all.'

Jody wanted to block her ears, and pretend she wasn't listening. But the facts were staring her in the face. There were poachers in the forest, and Sandhi was nowhere to be seen.

May 31 – early evening – at the Irrawaddy inlet
We've been waiting here for an hour, in case Sandhi comes back. Dad's worried about the poachers returning, but Mom and I wanted to stay as long as we could. The two males don't look worried, and there is no sign of a struggle along the riverbank, so those are good signs, I guess. Also, the boat doesn't seem to have moved since we were last here. But I can't help thinking that maybe Sandhi has been snatched, caught out in the middle of the river or something. Oh, where is she? Why isn't she here?

Everyone was silent and worried as Philip steered the boat back out into the centre of the river. The light was beginning to fail, and it was important that they got back before the sun set and it was too dark to navigate.

Jody's mind was so full of worry for Sandhi, and frustration at not being able to remember whatever it was that was bothering her about the boat, that she didn't notice which route they were taking back to the rest house. Gradually, she realized that they were moving along a stretch of river she'd never seen before. With a sudden sense of unease, she remembered the breathtaking ride they'd had that morning, and how fast they had got home.

'Philip?' she asked hesitantly. 'Shouldn't we be back by now? Are you sure we're going the right way?'

Craig and Gina stopped their conversation, and looked up in alarm.

Philip was frowning, and studying the water. 'I think this is right,' he said doubtfully. 'We've passed the big mangrove tree that I usually steer by. Maybe the water just looks different. It's hard to tell after all the rain.'

Jody looked again. She was sure she would have remembered the snarled roots of a mangrove tree jutting out of the riverbank to her left. The roots snaked up out of the water in a big loop, causing little currents to jump and swirl around them. 'I've never seen those roots before,' she said.

Philip looked. 'Perhaps they've appeared because of the rain,' he suggested. 'The landscape changes all the time in this forest, Jody.'

'But the water levels have been rising, haven't they?' Jody persisted. 'And if they've been rising, surely any roots would be hidden by water, not revealed?'

There was no denying the logic of Jody's argument. They were lost.

Suddenly Jody noticed a crop of tall, straight bamboo on the riverbank to her left. It looked familiar. 'Over there,' she pointed. 'I'm sure that's the right way.'

'Do you think we should land, and think about this?' asked Gina, peering over the edge of the boat. 'We don't want to disappear into the forest for ever.'

Philip steered the boat towards the bamboo, and threw the rope over the stump of a mangrove tree at the water's edge. 'Now, we passed the large mangrove tree about ten minutes ago,' he began.

The bamboo rustled. Everyone jumped as a man suddenly appeared out of the undergrowth. With a sinking feeling, Jody recognized him. It was Mr Vikram.

'You again!' he shouted, shaking his fist at Jody. 'Didn't I tell you to go away from here and not come back?'

Craig put his hands in the air, confused. 'Excuse me, do we know you?'

Mr Vikram took a step towards the boat. Jody shrank back against the wooden seat.

'You are trespassing!' Mr Vikram yelled. 'Go, and don't come back!'

'Are you Mr Vikram?' asked Gina suddenly. 'We're lost, you see, and—'

Mr Vikram wasn't listening. He kept looking over his shoulder, back into the bamboo. Halfway through

Mr Vikram isn't pleased to see us . . .

Gina's explanation, he turned back towards her and spoke loudly and furiously in Hindi.

'Mom, he won't listen,' said Jody, tugging at Gina's sleeve. 'Come on, let's go. I think maybe I can find my way back from here – I came here with Shiv the other day, remember?'

'Yes, go!' Mr Vikram said rudely. 'And don't come back!' He turned and disappeared into the bamboo.

'Well,' said Gina, helping Philip to untie the rope. 'That must be the rudest man I've ever met.'

'Remember, his wife died last year,' Craig reminded her, as the boat pulled out and into the middle of the river again. 'We shouldn't judge him too harshly.'

'Maybe, but I don't think that's any excuse for behaving like that,' said Gina.

Jody stood with Philip at the helm of the boat, and helped him to steer in the direction she thought was the rest house. But something was wrong. She had a horrible feeling that they were still lost.

The sun was sinking rapidly, and the water blazed with red and orange reflections. Logs and pieces of wood torn from the trees in the storm floated past, making Jody think of crocodiles. She tried not to think about what might happen if they still hadn't found the rest house in half an hour's time.

There was a sudden familiar cacophony of whistling and clicking off the back of the boat.

'It's Susie!' Forgetting the danger for a moment, Jody scrambled eagerly to the back of the boat.

Susie, the long-beaked Ganges river dolphin, nodded and clicked at them, beating her tail from side to side and swimming smoothly up beside the boat. She dived and rolled and came back up for air, holding her beak straight out of the water.

'Did you know that Ganges river dolphins are effectively blind under water?' Gina told Jody. 'They find their way around using echolocation – vocalizing and measuring the echoes to judge the distance.'

'I wish this one would use its echolocation skills to get us home,' said Craig ruefully. 'I don't mean to scare you, Gina, but we still don't know where we are, and it's getting darker every minute.'

Susie swam off a little way, before turning back again towards the boat. She did this several times, clicking more and more urgently.

'I think she wants us to follow her,' suggested Jody, with a surge of hope.

'That only happens in films, Jody,' said Philip. 'Not in real life.'

'Let's follow her anyway,' Jody said persistently. 'She's going in more or less the direction we are. And she knows where we're staying, doesn't she?'

With a sceptical sigh, Philip steered the boat to the left and followed the dolphin.

'It does seem a bit unlikely,' Craig began, as the boat rounded a bend into a wider part of the river.

But Jody gave a triumphant shout. 'Look! *Dolphin Dreamer*!' *Thank you, Susie*, she thought fervently.

Craig and Gina sighed with relief to see the familiar shape of *Dolphin Dreamer*, silhouetted against the sunset and bobbing gently at its mooring by the Sukhi Rest House jetty. They were home!

Philip raised his hands in the air with a laugh. 'OK, dolphins can navigate!' he said cheerfully. 'I'll never underestimate them again.'

Susie surfaced beside the boat again and whistled loudly. Then she turned on her side, and swam off to the left, away from the boat.

'Look, she's waving,' grinned Craig as they

watched her go, one flipper trailing above the water.

It certainly seemed that way. Susie gave a final volley of clicks, and sank from view.

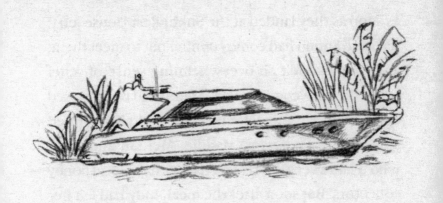

8

May 31 – almost bedtime – Sukhi Rest House
I wish I felt happier. It was a miracle that we found the
rest house after getting so lost, and it was fantastic to
see Susie again, but now we're back, all I can think of
is Sandhi and where she might be. Maybe she's in a
cage somewhere, or maybe she's already . . .

Jody snapped her diary shut with a determined shake of her head. She wouldn't give up hope, not yet. They didn't have any proof that Sandhi had been stolen.

The last rays of sun had faded from the sky almost

as soon as they landed at the Sukhi Rest House jetty. Ravi and Sunnu had come running out to meet them, and Jody had felt an overwhelming sense of relief to see their welcoming faces. Sunnu had then cooked everyone a large meal, and they had all swapped stories with Dr Taylor, Maddie, Mei Lin and Cam, who'd had a very interesting day with the local honey collectors. But soon after the meal, Jody had felt her spirits sinking as she thought about Sandhi, and had come up to her room for some peace and quiet as soon as she could.

Suddenly, Jody really wanted to talk to Shiv. He would understand how she was feeling. Putting her diary on the bedside table, she padded down the hall to Shiv's room. The curtains were shut, and a fan whirred gently in the darkness.

'Jody?' Shiv said sleepily. 'Is that you?'

'Good, you're awake!' Jody hurried over to him in relief. 'How are you feeling?'

Shiv switched on the light beside his bed, and yawned. 'A bit better,' he said, rubbing his head. 'My ankle still hurts and I think I got a bang on my head as well. But my mother knows how to treat a sprained foot. I will be walking again tomorrow, I hope.'

They both looked down at Shiv's foot, which had been tightly bound in neat, cream-coloured bandages.

'What have I missed?' Shiv asked. 'What did everyone say about the boat?'

Jody explained what had happened since Shiv's accident, and how the Kaushiks had told them about the poachers. She also described the return to the Irrawaddy inlet, and how Sandhi was missing.

'And then we got lost coming back, and to round it off, we bumped into Mr Vikram again,' she said. 'He was just as angry as before, of course.'

'Did you tell the others that you'd seen Mr Vikram in Mongla the other day, at the boatyard?' said Shiv, suddenly alert.

Jody smacked her forehead with her hand. Of course! '*That's* what's been bugging me!' she exclaimed. 'Something's been bothering me about the boat, Shiv – I felt like I knew something important, but I couldn't remember what. How could I have forgotten? We saw Mr Vikram in Mongla, buying a new boat! The boat at the inlet – it must be his!'

They stared at each other as this information sank in.

'Does that mean that Mr Vikram . . . is a poacher?' Jody said at last.

Shiv frowned. 'I don't think so,' he said. 'He is a strange man, but he is not a bad one. He's just unhappy.'

'But how do you explain that conversation we overheard at the boatyard?' Jody persisted.

'I don't know,' Shiv admitted. 'Maybe I didn't hear right. Let's go down and tell the others anyway.'

He started to get up, but Jody stopped him. 'You shouldn't get out of bed.'

'I'm OK,' Shiv insisted. He swung his legs over the edge of the bed, tested his foot on the ground and winced.

Jody reached forward. 'Here, lean on me,' she suggested.

Shiv draped one arm gratefully around Jody's shoulders, and hopped a few steps. 'That's fine,' he said. 'Come on, let's go downstairs. My parents can make a phone call to Khaled at the Mongla boatyard. He will know for sure if Mr Vikram was buying a boat.'

Very slowly, Jody and Shiv made their way downstairs. Jody was bursting to move faster, but she carefully helped Shiv down each step.

Jody's brothers and Shiv's brother and sister were already asleep, but the others were all gathered in the living area as they came in.

'Shiv, you should not be out of bed!' Sunnu exclaimed, jumping to her feet.

'We've remembered about the boat,' said Jody, helping Shiv into a chair and sitting down beside him. 'We think it belongs to Mr Vikram.'

Now she had the whole room's attention. She explained everything as quickly and clearly as she could.

When she had finished, Craig whistled. 'It certainly looks strange,' he said. 'Ravi, what do you think?'

Ravi stood up. 'I'm going to call the boatyard in Mongla,' he said.

'Isn't it rather late?' said Dr Taylor doubtfully.

'Khaled lives at the boatyard,' Sunnu explained. 'He will be at home now, I'm sure.'

'If the boat really is Mr Vikram's,' said Jody, 'do you think that proves he is a poacher?'

'No,' Ravi replied. 'It will simply prove that he is the owner. But it is a start. Now, can you describe the boat for me, Jody?'

Jody explained the shape and size of the boat as best she could. Craig and Gina added the colour of the leather seats and the tarpaulin. Best of all, Shiv came up with the serial number they had seen on the side of the boat.

'How did you remember the number?' Brittany asked in amazement, as Ravi went to make the call.

Shiv shrugged. 'It was easy,' he said. 'When you live with boats like we do, you remember things like that.'

They waited in silence. Jody tried to listen at first, but Ravi was speaking Hindi. She glanced at Shiv's expression, but he wasn't giving anything away.

At last, Ravi came back into the room. 'Khaled has certainly seen Mr Vikram recently,' he confirmed, looking round at everyone. 'Mr Vikram has just bought a new boat. With cash. He made the final payment and took the boat away with him, the same day that you were in Mongla. And the serial number matches the one you gave me, Shiv.'

'I knew it!' said Jody triumphantly.

'This only proves that he bought the boat,' Gina cautioned.

'But it's a start, as Ravi said,' Jody pointed out. 'Now we just need to speak to Mr Vikram.'

Ravi and Sunnu looked at each other.

'That is easier said than done,' said Ravi. 'Remember, he is not a very friendly neighbour.'

'I've got it!' said Shiv suddenly. 'Call him and invite him here tomorrow morning. Tell him you understand that we have been trespassing on his land, and would like to talk to him about it. He'll come, I know he will!'

The sun was beginning to appear over the tops of the trees the next morning when Mr Vikram came to the Sukhi Rest House. As Shiv had predicted, he had quickly agreed to come over for a meeting when Sunnu had called about the supposed trespassing. That small patch of bamboo-covered land was clearly very important to him.

Jody had been keeping watch on the veranda since dawn. She hadn't slept very well, her head full of anxious thoughts about Sandhi and the poachers. She had been quite relieved when the sun rose, and the dawn light began to filter into her bedroom. Brittany hadn't stirred when she crept out of bed and down to the veranda. She had made herself a cup of tea and had scribbled several pages of her diary before anyone else had got up.

Dr Taylor had been the first to appear. He was off on a bird-watching trip to the coast, with Mei Lin and Maddie. After she had waved them off, Jody had chatted to Harry and Cam aboard *Dolphin Dreamer* for a while. And at last, Mr Vikram's small dinghy had come into view.

As soon as she saw the boat, Jody scrambled to her feet and flew into the house. Her parents, the twins and the Kaushik family were now up, and were making breakfast in the kitchen. There was still no sign of Brittany.

'Mr Vikram's coming!' Jody announced excitedly. 'He'll be here in about ten minutes, I think.'

'Well, we are ready for him,' said Sunnu calmly.

'As ready as we'll ever be,' agreed Ravi.

Jody ran back outside, and watched as Mr Vikram carefully manoeuvred his dinghy down the river towards the Sukhi Rest House. When he finally reached the jetty, he lashed his small, rather shabby boat firmly to one of the jetty uprights. Then he hitched up the knees of his pale linen trousers and climbed up on to the jetty.

'Good morning, Mr Vikram,' said Jody cautiously. Seeing him up close again brought back unpleasant memories of being shouted at.

Mr Vikram peered at her. 'Good morning, young lady,' he said. 'I am here to see Shivam's parents. Are they at home, please?'

What a strange question, Jody thought as she brought Mr Vikram into the rest house. Where else would Sunnu and Ravi be at this time of the morning?

Mr Vikram seemed surprised at the number of people waiting for him inside. He hesitated briefly in the doorway.

'Mr Vikram, good morning,' said Ravi, stepping forward. 'Allow me to introduce the McGrath family. Mr and Mrs McGrath have come here to study the dolphins.'

Did Mr Vikram look nervous at the mention of dolphins? Jody looked closely, but his expression gave nothing away.

'I am very pleased to meet you,' he said formally, making a small bow.

'Do sit down,' suggested Sunnu.

'I prefer to stand,' said Mr Vikram. 'I hope this will not take long.' He shifted slightly, clasping his hands behind his back. Jody decided that he reminded her of a tall, rather awkward-looking heron.

'I am here to discuss your son,' continued Mr Vikram. 'I would appreciate it if he would stay away from my property. Can you give me your promise that he will do so?'

'We don't want to upset you, Mr Vikram,' Ravi said. 'I think there has just been a misunderstanding about who owns the land. Of course, if Shivam is trespassing, we will speak to him about it.'

Jody looked around, but Shiv was nowhere to be seen.

Mr Vikram seemed at a loss quite what to say next. 'I would like your promise,' he said again. 'If you please. It is your role as parents to control your children.'

The sound of laughter echoed from the direction of the jetty. Shiv, Ajay and the twins were obviously playing outside.

'We can only apologize, Mr Vikram,' said Sunnu.

'I'm sorry if Shiv has been a nuisance for you.'

Ravi cleared his throat. 'There was something else we wanted to discuss with you, Mr Vikram,' he said politely. 'It is a small matter of a boat. A new boat we have found, moored some way up the river. We have reason to believe it is yours.'

Mr Vikram suddenly looked wary. 'A boat?' he asked. 'I have my only boat outside.'

Ravi shook his head. 'I have spoken to Khaled at the Mongla boatyard,' he said. 'We know that it is yours, Mr Vikram. And we think that maybe you know something more. Perhaps something about the poachers who have come to this area?'

Mr Vikram quivered with anger. He drew himself up as tall as he could, and stuck out his chin. 'I have no new boat!' he declared loudly. 'I know nothing about poachers. I do not like your questions, and I now believe that you did not bring me here to talk about your son at all. I do not appreciate being tricked!'

With those words, he swung round quickly and marched out of the rest house door.

'Oh dear,' Sunnu muttered, collapsing into one of the armchairs. 'I think we have offended him.'

No escape . . .

'I think we have scared him, more like,' said Craig grimly. 'Did you see his face? Quick, we have to bring him back!'

They didn't have to go very far. Mr Vikram was standing on the jetty, staring in disbelief at the empty place where his boat had been. Out in the middle of the river, Shiv was waving, a broad grin on his face. He was bobbing gently in Mr Vikram's boat, along with Ajay, Jimmy and Sean.

Craig ran up to Mr Vikram and touched his arm.

Mr Vikram roughly pulled away, looking fearfully into Craig's eyes.

'Please, Mr Vikram,' said Craig gently. 'We are not accusing you of anything. We simply want to know if the boat is yours, and if you have noticed anything strange in the area recently.'

Jody held her breath.

Mr Vikram suddenly looked defeated. 'The boat is mine,' he muttered after a long silence. 'What of it? I have two boats. This is the Sundarbans. You must have a boat to live here.'

'Then why did you lie to us?' asked Jody, stepping up beside her dad. 'And why didn't you come here in your new boat, instead of your old one?'

Mr Vikram wouldn't meet her eyes. 'I don't know anything about poachers,' he said stubbornly.

'Is there a particular reason you don't want anyone near your land?' Craig pressed.

Mr Vikram hesitated. 'No,' he said at last.

'Mr Vikram, you must tell us the truth,' said Craig. 'We don't want to bring UNESCO into this, but I think that they need to know what is going on.'

Mr Vikram looked frightened. 'I don't want people

there!' he said passionately. 'I don't want . . . They will take them away!'

'Take who away, Mr Vikram?' asked Jody.

Mr Vikram crumpled in front of them. 'My tigers,' he said. 'My precious tigers.'

9

June 1 – morning – on the veranda at the Sukhi Rest House

When Mr Vikram mentioned tigers this morning, he surprised everyone. It's not really the kind of conversation you expect to have with someone you suspect of being a poacher! His voice was full of an emotion that I don't suppose poachers know much about – love. I recognized it straight away because it's how I feel about dolphins. I sometimes feel like I'd jump in front of a firing squad before I let anyone hurt a dolphin. I got the feeling that Mr Vikram felt exactly the same about tigers. And suddenly, I decided that I liked him.

M r Vikram buried his face in his hands, shaking his head helplessly. A few tears trickled through his fingers, and splashed on the jetty.

'Tigers?' Ravi repeated. He sounded astonished. 'What have tigers got to do with this?'

Mr Vikram just shook his head, over and over again, and kept his face covered with his hands.

'Come inside, Mr Vikram,' Sunnu said gently, laying her hand on his sleeve. 'Come and sit down.'

'Good idea,' said Gina. 'Let's have some tea, and talk about this. There's a lot more to this situation than meets the eye, I think.'

Mr Vikram had no more fight left in him. Meekly, he followed Sunnu and Ravi into the house.

'Are you arresting Mr Vikram?' Jimmy shouted excitedly from the boat.

'No,' Craig called back severely. 'But we're thinking of arresting *you*. Stealing boats, at your age! Come back into shore, boys. You've done your bit, I think.'

'Now,' said Craig, when they were all finally seated on the veranda and Sunnu had made tea. 'Do you feel up to telling us whatever is bothering you, Mr Vikram?'

Mr Vikram was slowly calming down. He accepted the tea Sunnu offered him, and he seemed to be thinking hard before he spoke. 'I am sorry,' he said stiffly. 'I am emotional today. It has been a very hard time for me.'

'You mentioned tigers,' Jody prompted.

The fear came back into Mr Vikram's eyes, and he looked down into his lap.

'My wife died last year,' he began. 'Perhaps you know this already. We had been married for ten years. The illness should not have killed her, but life had been hard for a while, and she was weak and tired.' He paused and swallowed. 'I felt guilty that I couldn't save her.'

'It wasn't your fault,' murmured Sunnu, her eyes soft with sympathy.

Mr Vikram shook his head. 'I think maybe that it was,' he said. 'My business was failing, but I refused to give up. The shellfish were disappearing from the river, but every day I thought we would make a big catch again, like in the past. Maybe we should have gone to Mongla, and I should have found work there. But my father and my grandfather had worked on the river always, and I was too proud to leave.'

'It has been a hard time for everyone in the Sundarbans,' said Ravi. 'Pollution, irrigation schemes upriver – the delta is changing for us all.'

Jody was suddenly aware, all over again, of just how much the people in the Sundarbans depended on the river for their livelihoods.

Mr Vikram was still talking. 'I was angry when my wife died,' he said. 'Angry with myself and angry with the world. So when the men came and offered me money, I took it.'

Jody felt a chill settle on her heart. 'Men?' she echoed quietly.

Mr Vikram looked at her. There was real sadness in his eyes. 'Bad men,' he said. 'I am ashamed now, but at the time, I felt nothing. They took animals with my help, and they paid me well.'

Thoughts of Sandhi's family rose in Jody's mind. But she pushed them down again. It was too late to help them now, she knew. Perhaps, by listening to Mr Vikram, they would still be able to help Sandhi and the others. What did this story have to do with tigers, she wondered?

'I found Aditi two weeks after the men left,' Mr Vikram continued. 'She is a Royal Bengal tiger,' he added, unable to keep the pride out of his voice. 'She was skin and bone when I found her trying to take food from my house. She was so weak and starving that she didn't even try to attack me. So I started to feed her. She helped me to get over the death of my wife, I think.' Mr Vikram stopped and stared out of the window. 'She started to trust me.'

'And Aditi is now living on that patch of land with the bamboo?' Gina asked.

Mr Vikram nodded. 'She is living there with her new family,' he said. He gave his first real smile. 'She had two cubs three months ago. I have been protecting her, and taking food to her – just to build her strength back up.'

'Is she the tiger we have been hearing these past few days?' Ravi asked suddenly.

Mr Vikram nodded. 'She has been calling loudly in the past week – calling for her mate, I think. It made me afraid.'

'But why are you afraid?' asked Gina in confusion. 'You know that she won't hurt you.'

Mr Vikram raised his hands in the air. 'I'm not afraid for myself, Mrs McGrath,' he said. 'I am afraid for Aditi. Because the poachers are back, and I know they want to take her away.'

'But are you helping the poachers again?' asked Ravi.

Mr Vikram looked ashamed. 'I don't want to,' he said helplessly. 'But they know about the tigers. If I don't help, they will take them away.'

'Blackmail,' said Craig. 'Right?'

Mr Vikram was silent. Then he nodded. 'The poachers know that I will help them in order to protect Aditi and her children,' he said.

'Did they give you the money to buy the boat?' asked Sunnu.

Mr Vikram nodded again. 'Yes,' he whispered. 'My business still isn't so good, so I have taken a little money from them.'

Jody suddenly felt heart-wrenchingly sorry for Mr Vikram. She wondered what she would do in the same situation, if Sandhi was in danger, and helping the poachers was the only way to protect her. Then she remembered that Sandhi was already in danger. Very grave danger.

'Do you trust these men?' asked Philip suddenly.

Philip hadn't been in the room the last time

Jody looked. Now he was leaning back against the doorway with his art bag and stool propped up beside him. He must have come in from painting while they had been listening to Mr Vikram.

Mr Vikram looked taken aback. 'Of course not!' he said. 'They are bad men. I would be a fool if I trusted them. Even more of a fool than I am now,' he added quietly.

'So what's to stop them taking your tigers anyway, even if you help them?' Philip continued.

Mr Vikram opened his mouth, but no sound came out.

'Philip's right,' said Gina. 'I think these men will try to take Aditi and her cubs, whether you help them or not.'

Mr Vikram jumped to his feet, and started pacing up and down. 'But what else can I do?' he said.

'We can help you to protect the tigers,' offered Jody. She looked at her dad, who nodded and smiled at her.

Mr Vikram slowly sank back down into a chair. He looked overcome at Jody's offer. 'You will help me?' he said. 'Even . . . even though I too am a bad man?'

'You are not a bad man, Mr Vikram,' said Gina kindly. 'You just made a mistake. Now you have a chance to make up for what you did, and help us to preserve the wildlife of the river.'

'But you must tell us everything you know about the poachers,' added Ravi. 'We must then involve UNESCO. This is a very serious matter. Do you understand?'

Mr Vikram gave a very small nod. 'Yes,' he said. 'I see that it is the only way. Very well. If you promise to help me protect Aditi and her family, I will tell you everything I know.'

At last, the whole story came flooding out. Mr Vikram explained that the poachers operated along much of the Sundarbans coast, preferring to move around rather than stay in one place for too long. There were three of them in the gang, and they stole animals of all kinds – crocodiles and snakes for their skin, monkeys for their fur, birds for their feathers, turtles and dolphins for their meat and oil. Jody felt sick to her stomach. She desperately wanted to ask Mr Vikram if the poachers had taken Sandhi, but she was afraid of the answer. So she stayed silent – until Mr Vikram made a startling announcement.

'They are meeting again tonight,' he said, looking round at everyone. 'At the boat.'

'Tonight!' Jody gasped. Suddenly, it all felt very dangerous and very real.

'Then we will be waiting for them,' said Craig grimly. 'They have got away with it so far. But tonight is our big chance. We'll call UNESCO, and tell the other people along the river. Do you think they'll help, Ravi?'

'Definitely,' said Ravi quietly. 'Men like these poachers are stealing from our river. We all want to stop them.'

'Then that's settled,' said Craig. 'Tonight it is.'

Jody stood on the jetty with her family and the Kaushiks, and watched Mr Vikram's boat as it headed back upriver.

'I think he is sailing his boat more happily,' Shiv observed.

Jimmy laughed. 'How can you sail a boat happily?' he said. 'That's stupid.'

'Shh, Jimmy,' Gina cautioned, putting her arm around him. 'I know what Shiv means.'

'So do I,' said Jody, watching the little boat's

progress. Mr Vikram turned and waved once, before the boat disappeared around the bend. 'Mr Vikram knows he's not on his own any more.'

Brittany came out of the rest house, yawning and holding a cup of tea. 'You're all up early,' she said.

'We've been pretty busy,' Jody grinned.

Brittany listened to the events of the morning with wide eyes, completely forgetting about her tea. 'So they're coming tonight!' she gasped, as Jody came to the end. 'But – won't they be dangerous?'

Sailing more happily . . .

'We'll be able to cope with them,' said Jody confidently.

Craig held up his hand. 'Stop right there, Jody,' he said. 'What's this "we" business?'

'Dad!' Jody began, but her heart was sinking. She knew what he was about to say.

'You can forget about joining us tonight,' Craig continued severely. 'It'll be far too dangerous.'

'Your dad's right,' said Gina. 'I'm sorry, Jody.'

'But that's so unfair!' Jody burst out. 'Shiv and I remembered about Mr Vikram and the boat. You wouldn't even know about the poachers if we hadn't remembered!'

'I want to come as well!' insisted Shiv.

'Me too!' added Sean and Jimmy in chorus.

'Me three!' That was Ajay. Jimmy had taught him the new expression that morning, and he was keen to try it out.

'We're very grateful to you and Shiv, Jody,' Ravi said, holding up his hands. 'But we can't allow any of you to come with us tonight. I'm sorry.'

It seemed that that was the end of the discussion. The adults returned to the rest house with Ajay, Ambika and the twins, leaving Jody, Shiv and

Brittany still standing on the jetty. Jody felt so disappointed that she thought she was going to cry.

'Don't be upset, Jody,' said Shiv. 'You know what grown-ups are like.'

Jody sighed. 'I know. I shouldn't be too surprised, I guess.'

'I can't believe you want to go!' said Brittany. 'I mean – they might have *guns* or something.'

'Hey, you three.' Philip had reappeared from the rest house, and was walking towards them. 'We've had an idea,' he said, when he reached them. 'I know it's disappointing that you can't come tonight, but I've got a suggestion. Something that might take your minds off the poachers.'

Jody didn't think anything would do that, until she heard Philip's next words.

'Why don't we go and feed Mr Vikram's tigers tonight instead?'

10

June 1 – early evening – on the way to Bamboo Island (new name!)

I can't write much, because the pages will get wet. The river's calmed down a lot since the storm, I'm pleased to say – but my writing's still a bit wobbly. We're heading for Bamboo Island with some dinner for the tigers. We collected the meat from Mr Vikram on our way here, and Philip put it right in the front of the boat. Shiv doesn't seem to mind, but Brittany is sitting as far away from it as possible. I can tell Philip's really excited. I guess he's finally going to see some tigers close enough to draw!

I'm trying to stay positive, but I keep seeing grey

shapes rising out of the waves, and thinking that maybe it's Sandhi. Feeding tigers is exciting, but I still can't stop thinking about the poachers. Will Mom and Dad be OK? They got a group of UNESCO patrol guys and a whole lot of the Kaushiks' friends together, so they've got plenty of back-up. Mr Vikram said that there were only three poachers, but what if they have guns, like Brittany said?

Jody closed her diary and put it in her rucksack. She was just getting more and more worried, and besides, they were nearly at Bamboo Island. Shiv was already standing up with the dinghy rope in his hands, ready to throw it over the old mangrove stump. Moping about Sandhi wasn't going to help, Jody knew. She straightened her shoulders and jumped ashore.

'I really hope these tigers are as tame as Mr Vikram said they were,' joked Philip, as he offered his hand to Brittany.

Brittany held back, looking uncertain. 'I think maybe I'll stay in the boat, just in case . . .' she began.

'Come on, Brittany,' Jody coaxed. 'Think of those lovely baby tigers. I bet they're really cute.'

Brittany's eyes softened. 'Do you think?' she said, stepping on to the island.

Jody half-expected Mr Vikram to jump out at them, like he had before. But the island was calm and still, with a gentle breeze swishing through the bamboo.

With the help of Shiv, Philip dragged the meat off the boat. They placed it carefully on a patch of ground close to the bamboo, as Mr Vikram had told them.

'It's disgusting,' complained Brittany, wrinkling her nose as she stared at the meat.

'Yes,' Jody agreed. 'But at least if we give the tigers some supper, they won't think about eating us.'

'Don't say things like that, Jody,' muttered Brittany, drawing well back from the bamboo.

Philip and Shiv joined Jody and Brittany on the shore, wiping their hands on their trousers.

'What now?' asked Jody expectantly.

'Now we wait,' said Philip, checking his watch. 'I hope they come soon. The light is fading fast. It would be just my luck to get close enough to a tiger to actually sketch it, but not be able to see it properly!'

'Do you think the tigers will stay still long enough

for you to *draw* them?' Brittany asked in amazement.

'A quick sketch, maybe,' said Philip. He then dug into his bag and pulled out a camera. 'And if they don't, at least I'll be able to get some real close-up photos,' he grinned.

Jody's eyes went longingly towards the river. Her parents and the others would be setting off soon. They would come past Bamboo Island on their way to the Irrawaddy inlet. She wished she could be with them . . .

'Jody!' Shiv whispered at Jody's elbow. 'Look!'

Jody turned to see the most amazing sight. A cautious orange and black striped face had appeared at the edge of the bamboo. Aditi the tigress stared at the visitors with a haughty expression on her face, as if daring them to come closer.

When no one moved, Aditi obviously decided that it was safe to come out. She padded out of the bamboo as gracefully as a dancer. Close on her tail were two young cubs, their orange and black fur soft and fluffy around their inquisitive little faces. One of the cubs batted Aditi's tail, and let out a small, high-pitched growl. The second cub waggled its fluffy behind, getting ready to pounce on its brother.

They were behaving just like playful cats back at home, thought Jody, entranced.

Aditi sniffed the meat slowly. The cubs yowled, hungry and impatient. With one last glance at the visitors, the tigress and her youngsters settled down to eat.

Jody looked across at Philip. He was wasting no time, and had already snapped several photos. Now he was drawing the tigers with swift strokes of his pencil. The tigers could disappear into the bamboo again at any moment, Jody knew. She fervently hoped that they would stay for a little while longer. She could hardly believe she was here, watching a family of wild tigers this close. Philip's pictures would really be something to add to the Dolphin Universe website. She could imagine how impressed her friends would be!

After twenty minutes, Jody heard the faint purring sound of a boat engine on the river. Was it the poacher patrol? She got to her feet as slowly as she could, trying not to frighten Aditi and her cubs, and walked to the edge of the island. Peering into the darkening evening, she saw a fleet of five boats heading towards her. Soon, she could make out her father, standing at the prow of the lead boat. She waved frantically, and was rewarded with a return wave and a smile.

Jody saw her dad lean down and whisper something to the driver of the boat. To her surprise, the lead boat peeled off from the rest, and headed towards her. In the boat were her dad, her mum, Ravi and two men she assumed were from UNESCO.

'Just thought we'd see if you were OK–' Craig began as they got close enough to Bamboo Island to have a conversation.

Jody hastily held her finger to her lips, and pointed at the feeding tigers. Five pairs of eyes widened as they met the fierce gaze of Aditi, who had looked up from the meat to examine the new visitors. No one moved for an agonizing minute. Then Aditi returned to her meal, growling softly in contentment.

'What a beautiful animal,' Gina whispered. 'I can't believe we're so close to her.'

Suddenly Aditi lifted her head again and looked behind her. She growled again. This time, her growl was less friendly. It made the hairs on Jody's neck stand up. Aditi had heard something she didn't like.

Her whole body tensed, and her cubs clustered nervously around her feet. The meat was forgotten. Something more dangerous was in the air.

Jody heard three voices speaking in Hindi. They were approaching from deep in the forest. Aditi and her cubs disappeared into the undergrowth, as silently as ghosts. Only the remains of the meat proved that the tigers had ever been there.

With a pounding heart, Jody looked across at Shiv. Three men, speaking Hindi. Could it be . . .?

'I think we're about to meet the poachers,' said Craig, his voice tense.

There was a rush of activity from the boat as Gina, Craig, Ravi and the two UNESCO men jumped ashore. Brittany gasped, and grabbed Philip's arm. Jody's legs suddenly felt like lead. Why were they here? Why weren't the poachers at the Irrawaddy inlet, with the boat?

'Get in your boat, now,' Ravi instructed them all. 'And stay quiet, OK? We'll handle this.'

Jody suddenly knew that this was for real. She ran to the boat, dragging Brittany with her. Shiv followed closely behind. The unthinkable had happened. They were about to meet the poachers face to face. How had this happened? They weren't supposed to be here! Had they come for the tigers?

Craig ran to the edge of the water. Jody watched as he waved at the remaining four boats, making urgent cutting gestures with his hand – *Cut the engines!* Quickly, the boats obeyed. In moments, the evening air was still. Very quietly, the four boats rowed into shore and anchored just off the island, ready for action.

The three men in the forest were approaching fast, crashing recklessly through the undergrowth. They seemed to be arguing with raised voices. Jody watched the unfolding scene with a sense of disbelief. This kind of thing happened in films, not in real life.

It was just as Mr Vikram had feared. The poachers had discovered Aditi's lair, and they were coming to get her and the cubs while Mr Vikram was waiting to meet them at the Irrawaddy inlet!

Jody watched from the safety of the boat as three men emerged from the bamboo, still arguing. One of them held a tranquilliser gun, and another had a long wire lasso. They were so wrapped up in their conversation that they were completely taken by surprise.

'Stop right there!' shouted one of the UNESCO men. He was holding a gun, and aiming it straight at the poachers.

The three poachers stopped dead. They stared at the reception committee in disbelief. Two UNESCO men from one of the back-up boats ran in and quickly disarmed the man with the tranquillizer gun. Soon all three poachers were on their knees, surrounded by men in official uniforms. Radios crackled as the patrol reported the arrest. Bamboo Island was suddenly swarming with officers, and the air buzzed with fevered excitement and relief.

'Got them!' Craig came bounding up to the boat with a broad smile on his face. 'Is everyone OK?'

'Yes!' Brittany shouted triumphantly. She punched the air with her hand. Shiv jumped out of the boat and ran over to his parents, who hugged him warmly.

Jody suddenly felt a bit trembly. Now that it was all over, she realized just how dangerous it could have been.

'Jody?' asked Craig. 'How are you holding up?'

'I'm glad you got them,' Jody said unsteadily, emotions welling up and threatening to overwhelm her. Then she burst out, 'But Dad, I'm more glad that you're safe!'

June 2 – morning – aboard Dolphin Dreamer
It's almost eleven o'clock already, and we only got up an hour ago. I think the excitement of last night wore us out. I don't remember much about the boat ride home, except that Mom and Dad were sitting next to me and holding my hands. It felt really strange coming back to the normality of the Sukhi Rest House. Everything felt so down to earth. I didn't even want supper. I just crashed out in bed. Brittany did, too.

So now we're all having a celebration breakfast aboard Dolphin Dreamer *– all the Kaushiks, Philip, the whole* Dolphin Dreamer *team and a few UNESCO guys. Mei Lin has made mango muffins, with some of Dr Taylor's fruit!*

I think we've met every single person in the Sundarbans today. They've all been dropping by, congratulating us and thanking us for our help. Mr Vikram didn't come, though. He told the police everything, and Dad said he probably won't go to prison.

He will need to go and stay in Mongla for the trial, though, so Philip promised to keep an eye on Aditi and the cubs. Philip's started a proper painting now, and he needs a whole load of new sketches. He won't have to rely on his photos after all!

I'm pleased that they've caught the poachers, obviously. But we still haven't found out about the one Irrawaddy dolphin I most wanted to see. Mom told me this morning to expect the worst about Sandhi, as stolen animals don't usually turn up again.

Jody stared out at the river, her diary open by her side. The sky was blue, and the water glinted and swirled around *Dolphin Dreamer* as she bobbed gently with the current. It was soothing to be on board again. They were planning to leave the Sundarbans in two days' time. Jody knew that there would be new adventures to distract her from thoughts of Sandhi and her family, but right now, she couldn't get excited about it.

Brittany came and sat next to Jody, holding two plates of mango muffins and banana bread. 'You're missing breakfast,' she said, offering Jody one of the plates. 'I had to fight Dr Taylor for these. He was going back for third helpings!'

'Thanks, Brittany,' Jody said. 'But I don't want anything right now.'

Brittany put the plate on the table. 'Well, it's there if you change your mind,' she said with a shrug. Then she got up and walked over to talk to Philip on the far side of the deck.

Jody turned back to stare at the river again, trying to ignore the cheerful chatter on the deck. A couple of crocodiles were sunning themselves on the riverbank with their mouths wide open. Several little birds stood beside them and picked at their teeth like small white dentists. Deep in the jungle she could hear the endless chatter and screech of the monkeys. The whole forest was alive. Now all she needed was for the small grey shape bobbing beside *Dolphin Dreamer* to turn magically into Sandhi, and the world would be perfect.

The small grey shape disappeared under the waves, then reappeared. Jody blinked and half rose from her chair. She stared into the water. There it was again! She had definitely seen a dorsal fin this time. She didn't dare let herself get too hopeful. Perhaps it was Susie the Ganges river dolphin? But

Sandhi has a surprise for me!

there was no sign of Susie's distinctive beak.

With mounting excitement, Jody pulled herself right up against the railings, and peered down into the water. One head, then another, smaller one appeared in the river.

'Mom!' she gasped. 'Dad! Shiv! Come quick! I think Sandhi's back!'

Gina came over. 'I told you not to get your hopes up, Jody . . .' she began.

'There!' said Jody, pointing. Happiness threatened

to choke her. 'It's Sandhi, see? And I think she's got a baby with her!'

Sandhi's grave little face bobbed up to the surface of the river. Beside her was the much smaller, paler head of a calf.

'It looks like the poachers didn't get her after all!' Gina breathed. 'She must have gone away to have her baby in privacy. What a clever mom!'

Jody stared deep into Sandhi's eyes. The dolphin's expression was soft and understanding, as if she knew that Jody had been worrying. *Stay safe, Sandhi*, Jody thought. *The poachers have gone now, so you and your baby will be fine*.

Her heart was full to bursting. Suddenly the merry chatter of the celebration breakfast aboard *Dolphin Dreamer* seemed perfectly in tune with her soaring mood. She'd never seen such a beautiful forest, or such lovely people, or such a gorgeous morning as this one. 'Where are those muffins?' she demanded, looking round. 'I'm starving!'

Sandhi bobbed on the surface of the river as everyone gathered around the railings of *Dolphin Dreamer* to watch her and her calf. She seemed to be enjoying the attention. In fact, her solemn little face looked like it would break into a smile at any minute.

You will find lots more about dolphins on these websites:

The Whale and Dolphin Conservation Society
www.wdcs.org

International Dolphin Watch
www.idw.org

Look out for more titles in the Dolphin Diaries series:

Book 1: ***Into the Blue***

Lucy Daniels

Jody McGrath's dolphin dreams are coming true! Her whole family is sailing around the world, researching dolphins – and Jody is recording all their exciting adventures in her Dolphin Diaries . . .

Jody can't believe her dolphin voyage has begun. A whole world of discovery awaits her aboard *Dolphin Dreamer*. But an unexpected passenger threatens to spoil the trip of a lifetime. And when a sudden storm puts Jody's life in danger, who can she turn to for help?

Look out for more titles in the Dolphin Diaries series:

Book 2: ***Touching the Waves***

Lucy Daniels

Jody McGrath's dolphin dreams are coming true! Her whole family is sailing around the world, researching dolphins – and Jody is recording all their exciting adventures in her Dolphin Diaries . . .

The McGraths are in Key West, Florida, visiting a very special dolphin centre – with dolphin teachers! Jody loves watching the dolphins at work. But then one of the teachers goes missing . . .

ORDER FORM

0 340 77857 1	INTO THE BLUE	£3.99	☐
0 340 77858 X	TOUCHING THE WAVES	£3.99	☐
0 340 77859 8	RIDING THE STORM	£3.99	☐
0 340 78495 4	UNDER THE STARS	£3.99	☐
0 340 78496 2	CHASING THE DREAM	£3.99	☐
0 340 78497 0	RACING THE WIND	£3.99	☐
0 340 84162 1	FOLLOWING THE RAINBOW	£3.99	☐
0 340 85116 3	DANCING THE SEAS	£3.99	☐

All Hodder Children's books are available at your local bookshop, or can be ordered direct from the publisher. Just tick the titles you would like and complete the details below. Prices and availability are subject to change without prior notice.

Please enclose a cheque or postal order made payable to *Bookpoint Ltd*, and send to: Hodder Children's Books, 39 Milton Park, Abingdon, OXON OX14 4TD, UK. Email Address: orders@bookpoint.co.uk

If you would prefer to pay by credit card, our call centre team would be delighted to take your order by telephone. Our direct line *01235 400414* (lines open 9.00 am–6.00 pm Monday to Saturday, 24 hour message answering service). Alternatively you can send a fax on *01235 400454*.

TITLE		FIRST NAME		SURNAME	
ADDRESS					
DAYTIME TEL:			POST CODE		

If you would prefer to pay by credit card, please complete:
Please debit my Visa/Access/Diner's Card/American Express (delete as applicable) card no:

Signature .... Expiry Date: ....

If you would NOT like to receive further information on our products please tick the box. ☐

Look out for more titles in the Dolphin Diaries series:

Book 3: *Riding the Storm*

Lucy Daniels

Jody McGrath's dolphin dreams are coming true! Her whole family is sailing around the world, researching dolphins – and Jody is recording all their exciting adventures in her Dolphin Diaries . . .

The McGraths have arrived in the Bahamas! Jody can't wait to pay a visit to Little Bahama Bank and see some Atlantic spotted dolphins – and maybe find out if the rumours about a lost treasure ship are really true . . .